MURDER, MYSTERY
AND MAGIC

An innocent man is arrested for a murder committed by a woman . . . A guilty man confesses to another murder — but the police arrest an innocent woman! A man finds the woman of his dreams — and finds he's in a nightmare . . . The tenants of a new block of flats are so delighted with their new home that they don't really want to go out — little realizing that they *can't* leave. Strange incidents from macabre stories of *Murder, Mystery . . . and Magic*.

Books by John Burke
in the Linford Mystery Library:

THE GOLDEN HORNS
THE POISON CUPBOARD
THE DARK GATEWAY
FEAR BY INSTALMENTS

JOHN BURKE

MURDER, MYSTERY AND MAGIC

Complete and Unabridged

LINFORD
Leicester

First published in Great Britain

First Linford Edition
published 2012

British Library CIP Data

Burke, John Frederick, *1922* –
  Murder, mystery and magic. - -
  (Linford mystery library)
  1. Detective and mystery stories, English.
  2. Large type books.
  I. Title II. Series
  823.9'14–dc23

ISBN 978–1–4448–1112–4

Published by
F. A. Thorpe (Publishing)
Anstey, Leicestershire

Set by Words & Graphics Ltd.
Anstey, Leicestershire
Printed and bound in Great Britain by
T. J. International Ltd., Padstow, Cornwall

This book is printed on acid-free paper

1

Agent's Cut

My secretary has always been very good at fending off importunate authors hoping to bluff their way into my office clutching armfuls of typescript for which they were sure I could negotiate a profitable deal with some distinguished publisher. But just before lunchtime this one incredible day she put her head round the door looking pale and worried, unsure of how she ought to have coped.

'David, there are two . . . two men here to see you.'

'I'm sure you can give them a thorough vetting, Maisie, before — '

'They're policemen.'

They were in fact two plainclothes officers: a Detective Inspector Emerson and a detective constable whose mumbled introduction escaped me.

'Mr. David Milburn?'

'The name's on our plate by the door.'

It was a silly, nervous thing to say, with no reason for being nervous. We surely weren't going to be accused of handling pornography or terrorist propaganda?

'Your agency represents Mr. Crispin Brooke?'

'It does.'

'When did you last see Mr. Brooke?'

'I had drinks with him and his wife last evening. Why? Is anything wrong?'

'You said with Mr. Brooke and his wife?'

'Yes. We were celebrating acceptance of his latest novel.'

'That's odd.'

'What's odd? It's quite common for old friends to get together when a deal's been pulled off.'

'Of course. You were friends as well as business acquaintances?'

The sun was warm on the window, but somehow a chill draught had begun fingering its way into the room.

'Of course we were. I mean, we are.'

The detective inspector smiled a very disturbing smile, as if he had caught me

2

out in some damaging admission.

He said: 'So you are not aware that Mr. Brooke died last night?'

It was not just a draught now, but a freezing pain in the guts. I could hardly breathe. 'Died?'

'And you must have been the last person to see him alive.'

'No, that's not so. Gemma — Mrs. Brooke — she must have been the last one. After she had dropped me off and gone back — '

'Dropped you off, Mr. Milburn?'

I stammered out a sympathetic tale of Crispin having perhaps had too much to drink, so that I decided to leave early and his wife had driven me home and then must obviously have hurried back to see how he was.

Detective Inspector Emerson took his time, as if savouring something in his mouth, chewing on it and liking the taste better and better, yet at the same time frowning at something far from tasteful.

'But that's rather odd, Mr. Milburn,' he said at last. 'Because Mrs. Brooke assures us she wasn't at home yesterday. She was spending the night with a friend, and knew nothing about her husband's death until she went home this morning. And then notified us. It was a great shock to her.'

* * *

I had been Crispin Brooke's literary agent for five years, and his wife's lover for three weeks, when she began to confide her worries about him.

'He's so depressed. Moaning all the time.'

She sounded cheesed off rather than sympathetic. Gemma was a languid woman with an oddly flat, passionless voice. This chill was one of the exciting things about her. It was a perpetual challenge to try and stimulate that exquisite yet unresponsive body. When she did respond, she went through all the right motions; yet one had the feeling that somewhere within that flawless ivory flesh, behind those slack and languorous lips, she was in danger of yawning.

I had not so far been so tactless as to ask how she got on with her husband.

4

After all, he was my client and we were supposed to be friends. But presumably she wouldn't have come to bed with me if she hadn't found him lacking.

Crispin's career had in fact been going downhill for quite a time now. Publishers had lost interest in his work. There were new names; new fancies; new voices squealing in the Groucho Club; new reviewers with backs to be scratched; and Crispin wasn't one of this clique.

It was a warm afternoon, and Gemma was lying back with a thin trickle of sweat glistening between her breasts. 'We've got to do something,' she persisted. 'I can't take much more of his miseries.'

I would rather have talked about something else, or drowsed for a while before we had the second bout. Mixing business with pleasure — particularly when it was her husband's business — did seem in bad taste. But I supposed we'd have to tackle this question sooner or later.

'I'm sorry,' I said. 'I do my best. But he's out of fashion.'

'He writes just as well as ever, doesn't he?' That level tone might have been

5

taken to mean that she never bothered to read any of his work, and was asking only out of curiosity.

'Publishers have changed. The market has changed.'

'I don't believe most readers want this modern rubbish. Every book jacket nowadays might as well have a photograph of the author's navel on it. That's all they ever seem to contemplate.'

I heaved myself up on one elbow and contemplated her navel; and then the rest of her. She wasn't all that many years younger than Crispin, but her skin and shape were those of an unravished teenager. Perhaps until recent weeks she hadn't been ravished all that often: although she never spoke about it, I was beginning to suspect that Crispin wasn't terribly active between the sheets.

Or maybe she couldn't be bothered to encourage him. The icy calculation in her eyes and her movements might put many a man off. I should count myself lucky she had decided to indulge in some variations with me.

Odd, for a man of action like Crispin to

be inactive in this one field of operations?

After leaving the SAS he had made his name with tough adventure stories.

For a long time they were tough enough and controversial enough to satisfy the public. But as time went on he had used up all this authentic background material, and his imagination wasn't inventive enough to save his fiction from contrivance and repetition. And when he attempted to introduce a bit of obligatory sex into his stories, it came out laughable.

I looked down into that disconcertingly cool face and said: 'Is this why you've been coming to bed with me? Simply to coax me into fiddling things somehow for your husband? To get me under your thumb?'

She smiled her listless smile. 'Not just my thumb.' She pushed my arm away and rolled over on top of me. Her eyes were closed — in bliss, or sheer indifference?

We forgot about Crispin for a few minutes. At least, I did. But the moment we had finished, and she had uttered that half-contemptuous laugh with which she always rounded off a coupling — insulting in a way, yet provoking a vow that next time I'd make her gasp rather than laugh — she murmured in my ear: 'I mean it. We really do have to do something about him. Otherwise I'll finish up pushing him off a bridge or something.'

It was nearly time for me to get back to my office and for Gemma to go out and finish her pretence of shopping.

As we dressed, I said: 'Look, I've got his last two typescripts on my shelf. They've both been round six publishers, and they're getting very dog-eared. Rather gives the game away.'

'You can have fresh copies run off, can't you? Or get them sent out on line, or whatever they call it nowadays. And charge him against his next royalties.'

'If any.'

She looked back over her shoulder and shrugged that shoulder as if deciding that I too was a washout. I couldn't help snapping back: 'No matter how we tart either of them up, there's precious little chance of an acceptance.'

She reached for her tights. She really did have the most beautiful back; and she was moving her hips most tauntingly, as if to demonstrate what I'd be missing if I didn't come up with some bright idea.

It couldn't just be that she wanted to stop Crispin moaning and boring her. She must think more of him than I had guessed so far. In which case, why was she here with me?

Using me. But that back, those shoulders . . .

'All right,' I said. 'There might be one way to ensure publication.'

'About time, too. I knew you'd come up with something.'

'You pay to have your own book printed and published. Handle your own distribution. Or pay some firm to handle the lot — printing and distribution. Vanity publishing, they call it.'

'How much would it cost?'

'More than it's ever worth.'

'How much?'

'Now, just a minute. Crispin would hate it. No way would he admit that he had to —'

'He doesn't need to know.'

This was surely way out of character. 'You'd really do that for him?'

'He's been a good breadwinner so far.' She sounded resigned rather than grateful. 'We've got to keep him ticking over.'

'Wouldn't that sort of payment show up somewhere? I don't know how the two of you manage your budgets, but surely he'd be bound to notice?'

'He leaves the handling of the books to me. *Those* sort of books. I was his secretary, remember?'

I was tempted to ask her if she really loved him that much, but it didn't seem quite right at the moment. Or maybe any other moment.

I always hated this stage when all that sleek beauty disappeared within an everyday dress: smart and expensive, but still only an unremarkable sheath for such remarkable contents.

'Next Tuesday, then?' she said levelly. 'And you'll let me have all the details then?'

'Now, look, I'm not sure — '

'Rather than some vanity publisher, as you call it, couldn't you approach a reputable one? Someone glad to do you a favour?'

'Favours come with a high price tag in this business.'

'I'm sure you can manage it, David.' She stooped to look in the dressing table mirror and pat her already trim hair back into its tight, boyish helmet. As if peering through the glass at someone she had just recognized, she said: 'Wasn't there that rather interesting woman you introduced me to at that last party?'

'There've been so many parties. The only one you came to without Crispin — '

'Nina. Wasn't that it? Nina something-or-other. She seemed rather nice. And quite fond of you.'

'Nina Whiteley.' I didn't think Nina had ever been all that fond of me, except when I brought her a potential bestseller; but now I did recall that she and Gemma had talked enthusiastically together for quite a time. 'A very agreeable contact,' I conceded, 'but she's already rejected those last two books of his.'

'But with adequate financial back-up to cover any losses, couldn't she be persuaded?'

'Are you serious about this? I mean, if

anything went wrong, as it well might, Crispin would kill you if he found out.'

It was only a turn of phrase, but for a moment her eyes gleamed with an excitement I'd never aroused in her before. Her lips seemed to mutter the words silently. *Kill me . . . kill . . .*

Aloud she said: 'Tuesday.'

She clung obediently to me while I kissed her goodbye, and smiled her frigid smile. It was routine. With the usual post-coital *tristesse* I found myself thinking that all she really wanted was attentiveness rather than passion.

Gemma left by the back door of the block into the gardens. I waited ten minutes as usual, before going out and hailing a cab to take me back to the office.

At my desk that afternoon I was awash with doubts about her ideas on Crispin's behalf. As a conscientious professional agent, I disapproved of the basic amateurism of vanity publishing; and on top of that there was something about Gemma's whole attitude that gave me the shivers.

But by the next day I was already so hungry for her naked in my arms that I knew I had to act. I wasn't going to risk facing her on the Tuesday and telling her I'd decided I couldn't go ahead with the scheme. Would she be capable of turning, expressionless, and walking out?

All too possibly. So I went to see Nina Whiteley.

*   *   *

'Yes, I do remember her,' said Nina. 'Charming girl. Never met her husband — that client of yours, right? — but I couldn't help wondering . . . '

Not wanting her to speculate too far, I said: 'I've got a couple of propositions.'

She settled herself in her chair with that cheerful scepticism which so many agents and authors had had to face. The challenge was to break it down, or fail; to argue with her, or woo her.

I had never found it easy to woo Nina. She was thin, dark-haired, and had a darkly bossy manner, as if in dealing with men she had to be as masculine and menacing as possible. There was talk of a divorce in the distant past, but the word

'Mrs.' never crept into correspondence or into the gossip columns of the literary supplements.

I said: 'I've been thinking you ought to have first look at a project one of my clients is working on.'

'Anybody I've heard of?'

'He's collaborating with a certain politician's dumped doxy who has quite a tale to tell. Several tales, in fact.'

'You mean ghosting.'

'The collaboration is a bit closer than that.'

'Tell me more.'

Her immediately receptive attitude was unusual. As a rule, her studied indifference was part of the game, waiting to see if the next move was worth following up or should be wiped off the board

I told her more. About the revelations, political and personal, the minister's discarded mistress was telling to her new lover — a journalist who had done many skilful interpretations of governmental scandals and was always eager to broaden his collection of misdeeds. There was also a hint — I wasn't going to admit to more than a hint at this stage — of some slightly kinky involvement of another woman in the new ménage. At intervals Ms. Whiteley nodded, as if to hurry me along and get down to the real business — which I assumed would be the usual wrangle over royalties, advances, availability of the key people for interviews and publicity and so on.

When I had finished and, to my surprise and delight, she had expressed readiness to conclude a deal as quickly as I wanted, I said: 'And now I've got a favour to ask.'

'I've already done you a favour, buying your project.'

'No, I've done *you* a favour by giving you first offer.'

She smiled and crossed her long, lean legs. She really was in a good mood this morning. I wondered if she was having an affair, and was still purring over the pleasures of the previous night. But her attention did seem to be entirely on what I was saying.

'Why don't we have lunch together?' I suggested.

I quite expected her to say that she was tied up that day — it was pretty short notice — but she said: 'Why not?'

Over a cool, scintillating Sancerre I put the proposition to her. In return for the rewarding deal I had just done with her, would she be prepared to publish a subsidised edition of Crispin Brooke's latest novel? Yes, I knew she had already seen both of the more recent ones, and rejected them; but one hadn't been all that bad, had it?

'Not all that bad,' she granted, 'but not all that good.'

'But it wouldn't actually disfigure your list.'

'No. Only it wouldn't be likely to sell many copies. Precious little return for our money. Our accountants wouldn't like that.'

'It's not *your* money I'm talking about. Accountants don't get too cross if income is guaranteed before any expenditure has to go out, do they? Crispin's wife is offering to underwrite the book. Just so he can see his name in print again. To give his friends autographed copies. You know what authors are like. That's all we have in mind.'

'We?' She swilled the wine gently round her glass, and the word round her palate. 'David, just what terms are you on with Mrs. Brooke?'

'I'm . . . well, she's Crispin's wife, we've all been good friends, she's . . . well, naturally I see quite a lot of her.' I didn't dare lift a suggestive eyebrow.

There was a long silence. I thought she was marshalling arguments against the proposition, but in the end she said: 'I'd rather like to meet her again. Talk this over with her, personally.'

'Is that necessary? I can act for her, the way I act for her husband.'

'Then you can arrange an appointment for her in my office.'

★ ★ ★

On the Tuesday, Gemma made no move to undress until I had told her the result of my meeting. Then she stripped with methodical deftness and settled obediently on her back.

When we had finished she said: 'Thank you, David.'

I didn't suppose she was offering gratitude for my physical prowess. She simply wanted to take up the conversation where we had left off.

'Has it occurred to you,' I asked, 'that if Crispin cheers up, he may get demanding again? Maybe you'll find yourself with a reinvigorated lover.'

'Would you be very jealous?'

It had never occurred to me until now. 'I . . . I don't know.'

'I don't think we're taking too great a risk,' she said.

A reverberating note of contempt had crept into that usually level voice. It was quite frightening hearing her virtually write her husband off as inadequate — and this at a time when the two of us were conniving to salvage him.

Trying to keep it light-hearted rather than dig too deep, I suggested that the best system would be for me to pay the total amount direct to the publisher, while Gemma could make regular payments to me in order not to knock too sudden and obvious a hole in the Brooke bank accounts.

'You can make regular visits here,' I

said. 'And hand over the instalment for my services. Give you an extra *frisson*.'

She smiled thinly. 'If it were about that sort of thing, shouldn't you be paying me?'

'That would muck up the whole plan. Anyway, better for you to regard me as a gigolo than for me to regard you as . . . well . . . '

'Do stop talking rubbish.'

We did stop talking for a while. She had got her way, so I could have mine.

I then told her that Nina Whiteley would like to meet her again. And suggested that we should both go along. Gemma, very cool and offhanded, said she would prefer to handle it on her own.

'Look,' I said, 'this isn't just girl-to-girl chat, you know. Not with Nina Whiteley. She's tough. A real butch lady at heart. Not safe to tangle with her unless you've got good back-up.'

'I'll tell you later how it goes,' she said with dismissive firmness.

We made love again. Or, rather, I made love and Gemma let me. But, again surprisingly, when we parted she kissed me more fervently than usual — yet with a bit of an effort, I sensed — and said: 'You're really not bad, David.'

Not bad . . . at what, specifically?

★　★　★

Crispin was complacent rather than grateful when I called him to announce that I had found a buyer for his *Dummy Run*. He has always assumed the attitude of a strong, silent man of action. 'About time, too. Glad they've come to their senses at last.' His tone of voice was the equivalent of a condescending pat on the shoulder. One of his NCOs had at last come up to scratch.

I imagined him being just as taciturn and doing things according to a strict discipline when making love to his wife. That might go some way to explaining Gemma's own unyielding face and voice even when her body was at its most yielding. *Lie to attention . . . at ease . . . wipe that smirk off your face . . .*

Not that I very often let myself think of the two of them together. It wasn't a picture I enjoyed.

Would you be very jealous?

The next time we were together I deliberately made her whimper. She had spent a lot of time in the bathroom before coming to bed, and her face looked set and almost hostile. She stared up at me with something I could almost have interpreted as revulsion. So I made it a bit rough, until she uttered that little moan of protest.

Having got her way over the deal to save Crispin's pride, was she going off me?

I said: 'How did you get on with Nina?'

'She's delightful. A truly strong character. Beautiful.'

It wasn't a word I would have used myself. Striking, yes. Strong, when it suited her, indeed. But beautiful?

'Well, it's all settled now, anyway,' I said. 'You don't need to get too involved. From now on you can leave it all to me.'

'Oh, but we're having dinner together next week. We've got so much in common.'

'I'd never have thought so.'

'You could say she regards me as part of the package.'

21

'Look, are you trying to cut me out?'

'You'll continue to get your usual percentage.' It came out as a cool, matter-of-fact insult. 'Your usual cut.'

I tried to keep things going my way. 'Speaking of which . . . ' My fingers strayed over her in the familiar preliminaries. 'Time for some more of my perks.'

She flinched. 'Don't you think this is getting a bit of a routine? A bit repetitive?'

It wasn't good enough. Not after all the trouble I had gone through on her husband's behalf. She gritted her teeth — I actually heard her do just that — as I mounted her; and when I lay back she said: 'So that's what rape is like.'

'Rape? For Christ's sake, Gemma, what's wrong?'

'You wouldn't understand.'

'Oh, I think I'm beginning to understand. You let me shaft you when you wanted me to do something for bloody Crispin. Now it's fixed, and I'm superfluous. Back to the joys of the marital bed? Back to normal?'

'It was never normal. Nothing like the real thing.'

'The real thing? Like what the two of us have just . . . ?'

'You wouldn't understand,' she said again, infuriatingly.

We parted very coolly. Early next evening, despising myself, I couldn't restrain myself from picking up the phone to ring her. Then at the last minute I put it down again.

Ten minutes later it rang. It was Crispin, inviting me round for a drink.

'We've just been talking about you. Gemma thinks we ought to have a little celebration. Tell you what, come round right now. Just for drinks.'

The invitation sounded stiff and oddly uninviting. Maybe Gemma's suggestion hadn't appealed to him at such short notice. I tried to argue, but at once he got into forceful mood and sounded down-right angry at any idea of my not doing as I was told. He might not really have wanted to offer one of the lower ranks a drink, but now that the offer had been made he expected it to be regarded as an order.

I rang for a taxi. If we were going to

knock back toasts to the revivified career of Crispin Brooke, I wasn't going to risk taking my own car and driving back awash with celebratory booze.

★ ★ ★

When I arrived, my discretion proved justified. Crispin immediately poured a large Scotch and stared at me as if to see whether I was man enough to knock it back. I had seen him in many moods — swaggering he-man, charismatic author at a signing session, and resentful, neglected author — but never in quite this tautly aggressive mood. If this was going to be a celebration, its atmosphere was no jollier than some of our dismal sessions discussing his falling sales.

Gemma swept in and kissed me more effusively than she had ever done before in her husband's presence or, for that matter, when we were alone together. 'Darling David,' she gushed. 'The miracle worker!'

She sat down, crossed her exquisite legs, and went on looking roguishly at me

— yes, roguishly — while Crispin without a word poured her a vodka and tonic.

There was a silence.

Gemma broke it. 'Crispin, do tell David about your idea for your next book.'

My heart sank. It would surely sound drearily the same as the theme of the last two. But for a moment he seemed to relax, and threw out a few vague ideas. Doubts and gloom had been banished. His present novel had been accepted and would come out later in the year, so what was there to worry about?

Yet he remained prickly and resentful about something.

I wondered how much more money Gemma was prepared to invest in their life together.

'A pity,' she said out of the blue, 'that you've never tackled a straightforward murder mystery. There's a market for them, isn't there, David?'

'If you've got the knack, yes.'

'Not my scene,' said Crispin dourly. 'Too much contrivance.'

Gemma wasn't looking at either of us but contemplating something far away.

'Isn't that the point? Working out a problem just for the fun of it. Dreaming up twists and turns, and then surprising everybody with a clear-cut logical ending. Aren't you even tempted?'

'Maybe you ought to try one yourself,' I suggested.

Now at last she glanced at me, with that same sudden gleam as when I had joked about Crispin killing her. 'Maybe.' It was an echo of that whisper: *Kill me . . . kill . . .*

And Crispin was glaring. Alert to any threat of competition as a writer? Or as something else?

Standing awkwardly in the middle of his own Persian rug, he emitted a bluff, would-be no-nonsense laugh. As if to show who was in charge here, he leaned down to kiss Gemma just as extravagantly as she had kissed me. Only I was sure his mouth didn't open. He kept his lips hard, compressed, assaulting. I saw her shiver.

'This last week' — he raised his mouth and spoke to me over her head — 'I've hardly seen Gemma.'

'Been out buying bottles of bubbly?' I

suggested feebly.

Gemma got up and, although the room was not particularly warm, opened a window which, I vaguely recalled, faced out across a passage between this house and the one next door. Then, not leaving the honours to her husband, she reached for the whisky bottle and insisted on refilling my glass. She took her time, leaning over me so that her left breast rested against my cheek.

Crispin glared at me. 'You're not really interested in my next book, are you?'

'Well, old lad, until you've come up with a few pages — '

'It's not me you've been interested in for a long time, is it? Not me or my work. It's my wife you're after.'

'Crispin, what the hell's got into you?'

'It's you. That's what. *You* getting into my wife. Every bloody day of the week. D'you think I'm blind and deaf and bloody stupid?'

I'd only been with her a couple of hours that one day in that one week. If she'd been away from home more than that, it wasn't with me. But protesting that it had certainly not been every day of the week would hardly have been a sensible defence. While I shook my head, playing for time, Gemma sat down again and looked coolly from one to the other of us as if to guess who might risk the first blow and who would qualify to carry off the prize.

I took it slow and dignified. 'I do think you'd find it more fruitful to keep your lively imagination for your writing, Crispin.'

'And don't patronize me, Milburn.' My Christian name had been ditched and his voice was rising to a parade-ground bellow. 'You've done damn-all to promote my books until even you could hardly fail to sell this last one. And all the time you've been having it off with my wife. Sniggering behind my back.'

'Where'd you get all these crazy notions?'

'From the way she looks, and the things she's told me.'

'Told you?'

Still Gemma wasn't saying a word. Might almost not have been in the room with us. Yet she was the most important person in that room, round which everything was revolving. Had they already had a big scene before I arrived? Was she planning to leave him? To come to me?

I put my glass down. 'I'm not going to listen to any more of this.'

'You'll listen to just as much as I choose to say to you.'

Now I was the one who was shouting. 'And who d'you think you are, insulting me without the — '

'How could anyone insult anyone as two-timing as you?'

I got up. 'I've had enough of this.'

'You're not leaving here until we've — '

'I shall leave here when it suits me. And it suits me right now. So just get out of my way, or else — '

'Or else what?'

He stood there, swaying from side to side. And we went on swapping ridiculous insults and accusations, standing in the middle of the room and making a racket like football hooligans. Enough, you'd have thought, to get the neighbours phoning or coming round and ringing the doorbell to complain.

I risked a glance at Gemma, hoping for a hint of some kind, wondering how

29

much she had really told him, or if that had just been a wild stab of his.

Her smile was distant, almost contemptuous — contemptuous, I thought, of both of us. Sitting there so silently, just letting it happen.

I said: 'I'm going to ring for a taxi.'

'Not from my phone, you're not. You can start walking. But only when I've finished with you.'

His threatening sway from side to side became erratic. He lurched forward, put out a hand, but could find nothing to grasp except my arm. I tried to steer him towards an armchair. He recovered for a few seconds, long enough to bellow a string of obscenities at me before collapsing into the chair.

In an undertone, hoping not to start him off ranting again, I muttered to Gemma: 'Look, how much did he have to drink before I got here?'

She seemed to wake up at last, and motioned me to follow her out into the hall.

'I do think you'd better go home and leave this to me.'

30

'But just what have you been telling him? What started all this?'

'Let him sleep it off. I can cope.'

'If you'd ring for a taxi for me, then. Don't want him to wake up and start another battle over his precious phone.'

'I'll drive you back.'

'I don't think that's a good idea.'

'I think it's a very sensible idea.' She had been so silent, and now was so decisive. 'Come on, David, I do know what I'm doing.'

She closed the front door very quietly, walked briskly but soundlessly down the short path to the gate, and then even more briskly along the pavement to the corner of the street. I had to hurry to catch up with her. 'Don't you keep your car in the garage?'

'There was somebody blocking the way when I got home today. Had to park it round the corner.'

When we were in her Mégane I said: 'You were talking about when you got home — home from where?'

'Shopping, of course. I do have to do some real shopping sometimes, you know.

Not just as a cover-up.'

She pretended to concentrate on the road, although there was little traffic and it was no more than a ten-minute drive to the block where I lived. We stopped a hundred yards from the entrance. That was unremarkable: we had always been careful to cover our tracks. Maybe we wouldn't need to from now on.

I said: 'Are you planning to leave Crispin?'

'We'll talk about that some other time.'

I put my hand on her arm. It tensed; and then she made too obvious an effort to relax. 'Are you coming in?' I asked. 'We can talk about things then. About everything.'

'The state he's in, I'd better get back.'

'The state he's in,' I said, 'you don't know *what* he'll do.'

'Oh, I think I know him well enough. Leave it to me, David.'

She kissed me quickly and meaninglessly.

'Tomorrow?' I said. 'I can take the afternoon off. Sort things out.'

'Tomorrow,' she said, 'maybe things will sort themselves out.' And as I got out of the car, she said with unexpected intensity: 'Thanks, David. Thanks so much for everything.'

★　★　★

So here I am in a police cell, refused bail. My solicitor has just left, and obviously doesn't believe a word I've told him, any more than the police do.

Their first assault had left me winded, incredulous. I didn't feel that I could really be in my own office, on an ordinary day, listening to something far more crazy than anything some of my clients offered as storylines.

'But hold on a minute,' I was protesting. 'She was there with us last evening. Having a drink. The three of us.' And when that stony face yielded no response, I demanded: 'Look, how did Crispin die? Fall over blind drunk, or something? Alcoholic poisoning?'

'Not alcoholic,' said the inspector. He cleared his throat and said very formally: 'Do you think we might come and have a look round your flat, Mr. Milburn? In your presence, naturally.'

'What on earth for?' I groped through memories of so many detective stories for the right procedure. 'Anyway, have you got a warrant?'

'If we have to get one, we shall get one. In the meantime, have you any reason to be worried about what we might find?'

I had no reason at all to be worried; but that didn't stop me being worried. There was something very threatening in the atmosphere.

And they soon gave me reason to worry. Once they had driven me home the two of them prowled from room to room with a hideous determination to find something where there could not possibly be anything to find.

'Look after things yourself, Mr. Milburn?' asked Emerson.

'I have a cleaner in twice a week.'

'Yes. All very tidy. Systematic. Do your own cooking?'

'When I'm not taking clients or publishers out,' I said as loftily as possible, 'or being taken out.'

'A very agreeable arrangement, sir.'

They peered about in the kitchenette, sifting my spice pots and condiments and jars of this, that and the other to and fro. It took a further fifteen minutes of trawling before the detective constable called from the bathroom to show the little phial tucked under the ball-cock of the lavatory system.

'Not alcoholic,' the inspector said again. 'A different kind of poison. Far quicker.'

It was grotesque. 'D'you seriously think I'd be clumsy enough to hide something, whatever it is, in such an obvious place? If I'd had anything to hide, that is.'

'In a hurry, last night? Going to tidy up when you'd got your breath back?'

'Last night.' I drew a deep breath and tried to keep my voice steady. 'If you ask Mrs. Brooke about last night, she's got to admit she was muddled. The shock of it, all right. Must have thrown her. She's simply got to confirm that we were there together, and she drove me home, and — '

'No, Mr. Milburn. Mrs. Brooke was away. She had gone to stay with a publishing friend. She was apparently scared of the hostility between her husband and yourself, and when she heard you were coming round she didn't want to be there.'

'A publishing friend?'

'A Miss Nina Whiteley. She went there for protection.'

A terrible, incredible suspicion was dawning. I thought of Gemma paying her usual quick visit to the bathroom that last time she was here. Thought of her strange silences and that recent conspiratorial expression of hers.

'Look,' I said. 'Exactly how did Crispin die?'

'Cyanide poisoning. And you wouldn't know that, Mr. Milburn? Even though there were only two glasses in the room, one of them with traces of cyanide. And both with fingerprints on which may just possibly turn out to be yours, Mr. Milburn.'

'And once we've had the stuff in this bottle analysed . . . ' His constable let the words hang in the air.

'I think we'll continue this down at the station,' said his inspector. And he began to recite the rigmarole I already knew off by heart, thanks to those client authors who went boringly through it every few chapters: ' ... but it may harm your defence if you do not mention, when questioned, something which you later rely on in court ... '

In the interview room my solicitor sat stony-faced beside me. For all the moral or legal support he gave, he might as well have been sitting alongside the policemen on the other side.

The accusation was that I had been pestering Mrs. Brooke, and on one occasion had raped her when she was visiting me to discuss her husband's work. She had made no complaint at the time because negotiations with her husband's publisher had been at a tricky stage and she did not dare to antagonise me. But then Crispin Brooke began to suspect, and had called me round that evening for a showdown.

'And you lost your temper, and there was a fight.'

'A fight? Me and Crispin? He was ex-SAS, you know. I wouldn't have stood a chance.'

'Neighbours confirm there was a shouting match. It could be heard halfway down the street.'

Of course. Gemma opening the window and then not saying another word that might give away her presence.

'As you say, Mr. Milburn, picking a direct fight with a highly trained soldier with the deceased's courageous record was risky. So in the end it had to be something subtler. If you can call cyanide subtle.'

'Cyanide's agonizing.' I knew that much, again, from my clients' fictional outpourings. 'He'd have screamed his head off.'

'Exactly. That, too, was heard halfway down the street.'

'But what time was this?'

Detective Inspector Emerson glanced at his sidekick, who studied his notes and said: 'About twenty-three fifteen, according to the neighbour two doors down.'

'But I was home by then. Gemma had dropped me off, and I was in the flat well before eleven.' I turned triumphantly to my solicitor, who stared dispassionately at the table.

'You have a witness to this, Mr. Milburn?'

'I've shown you, I live alone. But check on her car. Someone must have seen it parked round the corner from their house. Or dropping me off. She *did* drop me off.'

Then I went wild. I had been hoping that the nightmare could be driven away, that common sense would prevail, that Gemma would come to the rescue and somehow it could all be sorted out. But I knew starkly what had been going on; and I let fly.

Couldn't they see it? It was a put-up job. The two women — two lovers, damn them — had planned it from way back, maybe from that very first innocuous meeting.

Drawing two bloody stupid men into the trap. Despising us, wanting to get rid of both of us.

The taste in my mouth was as bitter as any poison. 'As a literary agent,' I said, 'I suppose I ought to have learnt to be cynical about such things.'

Part of the package: wasn't that what

Gemma had looked so smug about? She had gone to bed with me, suffered the indignity of something for which she had no appetite, gone through the motions . . . all the time saving her real self for her woman, her real lover.

'Crispin wouldn't have been likely to go along with a straightforward divorce.' I was trying to reason with those implacable faces. 'Least of all when it was something he'd regard as intolerably kinky. So it had to be a matter of getting rid of the obnoxious husband, and saddling another man with the blame. That way, Gemma inherits the royalties which have survived from those past successes, and she and the Whiteley woman can live happily ever after.'

'Very ingenious, sir.'

'You can't be that stupid!' I raged. 'You can't let them get away with it.'

'As a literary agent, sir' — the detective inspector took up my own words with a condescending smile — 'you must undoubtedly get a lot of tips from your clients on how to put a good story together. Right?'

'It's better than your other crazy

40

notion,' I protested. 'That one simply doesn't hold water.'

'I think we can promise you, Mr. Milburn, that by the time we've finished we'll guarantee to make it waterproof.'

★　★　★

Women. How did I ever let myself get pushed around by bloody women?

I wonder if Gemma or Nina will amuse themselves by taking it in turns to visit me in prison? Or simply cross me off their list altogether?

2

Please put me in a book

There used to be a time when no one from London ever thought of coming to live on our coast. Too cold for them. But now they're all at it — buying up weekend cottages and places to retire to. If you can stick the first six months, you live for ever.

That's what this Jeremy Craven fellow was told when he moved in. And put it straight away into one of his books. Hardly in the place, and already he was writing clever-clever things about folk who'd lived a lifetime here. And lecturing the Ladies' Flower Arranging Society and Rotary and the Young Wives and all that lot.

I went up to him after one of those talks. And I told him. 'You ought to put me in a book,' I told him. 'If I had the time, I could write it myself.' And then a couple of women came twittering round him, and he put on the charm and he'd got no time for me.

But I soon saw him again. In one of the local pubs. Got his own tankard by now, and calling the landlord 'Eric, old son.'

I asked him if he was interested in murder. He'd heard about the Senwich Common murder, hadn't he? It had been in all the papers. And of course most people still thought that half-baked young postman did it.

But I knew better.

I could tell him.

Then Eric leans over the bar and ruins it all. 'If Fred's telling you all about the murders he's committed, don't you pay him no heed. He's always having us on.'

So Craven props his elbow on the bar, and there's Eric grinning and telling him, 'Every time there's a death anywhere in Britain, off goes Fred to the station to confess.'

'Oh,' says Craven. 'One of *those*? Fascinating.'

And you know, he really did look

interested now, and I could see he was going to come over and patronise me — like the police do whenever I go and try to help them; or that doctor I was made to go and see. Well, I wasn't here to be laughed at. I downed my pint and went.

Next thing, he was off for a few months and I didn't slap eyes on him again till the end of the summer. I was walking past that little group of beach huts we've got at the north end, and suddenly he's standing in the doorway of one of them. Seems the Johnsons, who always go off to the Canaries for the winter, had given him the key.

He called me over, and he'd got a sort of greedy look in his eye; and he started nosing into why I felt this compulsion, as he put it, to go and confess every time there was a murder. He was so patronising, so damn sneering. I took it for as long as I could, trying to hint just that there were things I really could tell him if I wanted to, which I didn't. Then I found I couldn't stand the sound of his voice any longer.

There was a folded deckchair propped against one wall of the hut . . . and when I simply had to put a stop to that voice I did the only thing possible: I picked it up and bashed him over the head and went on bashing until he couldn't take any more and couldn't make any more of those silly wailing, grunting sounds.

Then I was very calm. Like some master criminal in a book — a *good* book, not one of *his*.

I had a look outside. Nobody about. So I tossed the chair into the sea and watched it being carried away. And I locked the door of the hut behind me and threw the key into the water as well. No one would find him till the Johnsons came back in the spring. No one would ask questions. He was a writer, he was always going off somewhere.

But after a week or so I couldn't bear the thought of him being in there, and nobody knowing I'd really done it this time.

In the end I had to go to the police station. The moment I walked in, the desk sergeant said: 'Here's Fred. Come to confess to killing Mr. Craven? Who tipped you off?'

I started in to tell him exactly how I'd done it, but he just snickered, that way he always has. And then I heard what the whole town knew by the evening: that Craven had been using the beach hut for . . . well, meeting a girl. A girl he shouldn't have gone near, a real bit of trouble. Anyone in the town could have told him that. And yesterday she'd gone down to let herself in, and found him — 'That's *her* story,' they all said — and someone heard her scream. But she'd done a fair bit of screaming ten days ago, in the pub with him, saying she had a good mind to beat his brains in. And the hut was plastered with her fingerprints. And she said she hadn't done it, and there were lots of things the police weren't happy about, but some of Craven's things were found in her bungalow, and anyway she's coming up for trial.

And they won't listen to *me*.

You know what it'll be like. Some

newspaper'll pay for her defence, just for the exclusive story, and then someone'll come along and write a book about her.

It's not right. What about *me*?

I'm the one who ought to be in a book.

3

Desirable residence

It was perfect. It had been planned to be so, and perfect it undoubtedly was.

You came back from the office or the laboratory or the works in the afternoon, and the place was waiting for you. It drew you in and welcomed you home. The main doors opened automatically as you approached, and the spacious entrance hall beyond was warm in winter, deliciously cool in summer. The lift was waiting. Before you went up to that beautiful flat on the twentieth floor, you punched a chosen sequence at the cuisine panel. There would just be time to get home, have a shower, accept a drink from the dispenser, and the tireless analytical brain in the depths of the building would have employed its electronic circuits to provide your meal in the delivery hatch.

If you were one of the lucky ones,

maybe you didn't even have to leave the building to get to your work. Perhaps you went into one of the office suites, or the shops on the ground floor. In that case this gleaming erection was a world in itself for you.

The only part you didn't know much about yet was the community hall. It was a magnificently designed room, and no doubt some impressive functions would be arranged there soon. But during the first few weeks, most of the inhabitants spent the time in their own flats, still delighted just by the idea of being here; sitting and thinking about it, or looking out of the window, or just sitting.

Yes, perfect. Standing away from the sprawling city yet within easy reach by mono-rail or helicar, it was the most magnificent specimen of its kind. You were proud to live in it. On one side fields and woods fell away into the green distance; on another, the outer suburbs of the city were hidden by a barrier of trees, broken only by the gleaming line of the railway. To the north was the helicar park, sleek and new.

There would be other palaces like this before long. Two more were already being rushed up a few miles away, their muscles being built in, the pounding heart and nerve centre delicately installed, the arteries woven into the framework. But this one here would always be the first, the great predecessor of the ultimate development. There had never been such a flawless *machine a habiter* before. Almost you felt that it lived and had a vitality of its own.

The people who were privileged to make their homes here were conscious of their good fortune. They felt that they and their neighbours added up to something special.

And they were right. For some time they did not know just how right they were.

* * *

Rafe Darby did not order a meal when he got home. Not tonight. He checked the information screen in the hall and checked on the shows that were on in town. Then he went up in the lift, helping himself to a cigarette from the ejector on the way up. His wife heard the door opening as he approached it, and was waiting for him when he entered.

'Hello, honey.'

He kissed her. 'I haven't fixed us a meal,' he said.

She stared. 'Why not? I'm hungry. If I've had one candy bar from the hatch while I've been waiting for you, I must have had a dozen.'

'You'll get fat and repulsive.' He kissed her again to prove that he was not convinced of this at all. 'What I thought was maybe we could hustle off up town and catch a show. There's a live one — a real old play, done live on the stage — at the ancient theatre in the Haymarket.'

It had seemed a good idea while he was on his way home. Now, suddenly, it wasn't such a good idea. He didn't really want to go out at all. Not any more. Funny, that. Now he felt tired, and it wasn't as though he had been overworked today. But there it was, he was tired, and he wished he hadn't suggested this theatre idea.

Fiona said: 'Look, honey, that's sweet

of you, but really . . . '

She was fumbling for words. She didn't need to. He was grinning.

'You mean you'd sooner stay at home?'

'Well, yes. But if you want to go — '

'Not on your life,' he said, thankfully. 'Not me.'

They ordered a meal on the personal service relay, and sat back to wait for it. Rafe yawned happily. Nothing like being home. It was queer that he should feel so listless when he got here, but it wasn't what you'd call an unpleasant sensation. He just sprawled back, and felt that somehow his energy was draining away, but there wasn't anything he wanted to do about it.

When the meal came they ate it and smiled across the table at one another.

'I'd much sooner stay home,' murmured Fiona.

'Me, too.'

Afterwards, they sat together and did not move. Once, Rafe made an effort to switch on the wall TV, but somehow he could not summon up the strength to do it. What the hell, anyway? Who wanted to see the same old faces, listen to the same old jokes, play the same corny guessing games night after night? He was sitting here nice and peaceful beside his wife, and that was good enough. Contentment, that's what this was.

Silence enshrouded them. Not a sound came up from the floors below; not a scrape, a thump, nor the sound of a voice filtered down from above. Of course the walls were soundproof. But this silence was due to something more than that. You felt instinctively that nobody was moving anywhere else in the building. If you opened the door of any flat and walked in, you would find the folk in there sitting just like this.

Rafe yawned again, and Fiona yawned with him. They exchanged smiles. They felt agreeably lazy, and at the same time virtuous — as though their tiredness were a result of working hard, of giving their minds to something useful and accomplishing something inexplicably beneficial.

★ ★ ★

Christopher Cardew sat at his desk and tried to make his pen move across the virgin sheet of white paper before him.

A lot of his friends considered that Christopher was a crank. The last romantic, they called him — or the last individualist, or the last eccentric, whatever epithet they felt in the mood for using to express their tolerant amusement and affection for him. A man who wanted to be a writer was an oddity in this century, when books were produced in such small quantities and then only for freaks and reactionaries; but to make it worse, he would not even use a cybernetic resolver, but insisted on writing his stuff out laboriously by hand.

And what stuff . . .

Right at this moment he was trying to express the thoughts he had had earlier in the day, when walking through the dark, cool-smelling aisles of the woods down there by the river. He had seen a small disused cottage and wanted to write an idyll about it. But the words would not come.

He sat back and looked round the

room. His wife, Lisa, smiled at him. She was exquisite, and he adored her. If he had not adored her, he would not have been here. It was Lisa who had insisted that they should snap up the opportunity of coming here to live.

'It will kill my work,' he had protested. 'The ultimate in artificiality . . . '

'Why you always condemn labour-saving devices as artificial, I can't imagine,' Lisa had said. 'And as for killing your work — why not regard it as a challenge? Why not show that your sense of traditional values' — she had got the jargon off pretty well by now — 'is in no way impaired by the oppression of modern technology. Let's live in a wonderful new flat and prove that we can still preserve our individuality.'

He had been quite unable to resist that, and so here they were.

And here was a blank sheet of paper.

For a moment he was conscious of a terrible fear. There was a sense of constriction that made him want to panic. He wanted to get up and rush out of this flat and right out of the building, clear away, out where a man could breathe.

But he did not do this. He let out a long sigh, and then it became a yawn. His strength, his creative power, his stubborn individualism . . . all ebbed away, were sucked away by something he could not comprehend.

His pen moved slightly between his fingers. He stared at it, puzzled. Now he knew that he was going to write, yet absurdly he did not know just what it was that he was going to write. It was as though the pen would guide his fingers. And that was wrong. Quite the wrong way round. But he continued to stare, offering no resistance, and slowly the pen began to scrape across the paper.

This, he wrote, *is the Manifesto of the Suprahomo. The time has come for the renunciation of petty selfhood and for the merging of individual human cells into a new and greater being. Only by a blending of talents and temperaments can true progress be assured. The future of the human race can be significant only if the selfishness of independent existence is abandoned and a new corporate awareness developed. We, the Suprahomo, hereby declare our intention . . .*

★ ★ ★

Mark Jordan, licensed telepath and detective inspector of the Central Investigation Bureau, was about to pay a call. An unofficial call. This evening he had done his five minutes of mental relaxation exercises, so that his telepathic faculties were smoothed down and brought under strict control; and now he was going to visit friends in this new building everyone was talking about.

Actually, he had expected to visit it a lot sooner than this. He and plenty of others in his Department had prophesied some fancy crimes breaking out right away in a place like that. They had been surprised by the quietness. Nobody was robbed, nobody took a poke at anybody, and — well, nothing at all happened. His first visit was going to be a social call.

He was curious about the place.

Envious, too, of the folks who had settled in here. He wouldn't mind a couple of rooms to himself way up at the top where those lights were gleaming, away from the congestion of the city. For him the city was a pulsing evil, something that could never be entirely shut out. Always there was the mental congestion, the ceaseless subconscious roar of several million minds, as well as the thunder of traffic. Out here he might find tranquility.

The doors opened for him. He entered, and they closed smoothly — almost obsequiously, you would have said — behind him.

He stared round the large hall. No boy came hustling forward, no bells shrilled. But suddenly a light winked to attract his attention. 'Reception,' said a suddenly illuminated sign. 'Visitor?' asked a smaller sign over a microphone.

He got the idea. 'Mark Jordan to see Mr. and Mrs. Cardew,' he said into the microphone.

Then he waited.

In less than a minute, Christopher Cardew emerged from a lift and came over to him, smiling awkwardly.

He said: 'Thought I'd come down to make you welcome.'

Queer. Mark found himself bristling. Something wrong. The probing, mind-searching faculty that he had deliberately dropped into abeyance flickered warningly awake.

'Nice place you've got here,' he said, with a foolish grin.

'I thought you'd like it.'

Mark was not trying to needle into his friend's mind. He didn't have to try; something came out right away. Chris had forgotten about this invitation. And now that Mark was here, Chris was sorry that the invitation had been issued.

Well, all right, Mark thought. All right, if that's the way it is . . .

He had a blurred vision of the Cardews' flat, and of their stillness and apathy. He felt himself rejected . . . and felt something beyond that rejection. It was frightening. It was too big to grasp for the moment, and as it took shape in his mind he knew that he had to get out of here.

He turned for the door.

'You're not going, Mark?'

There was swift alarm in Christopher's voice. His listlessness cracked and splintered as something thrust up from beneath it — something that was not Christopher at all.

Now Mark was moving — he was throwing himself at those doors through which he had come so smoothly and easily.

Not so easy to get out of them again. They were tightly shut, firm against his onslaught. And all about him he felt the alarm being given, the warning shouted silently throughout the building.

Someone came out of a door at the far side. A lift sighed down close to him, and there were more men coming at him. They had strangely blank faces, but their clutching hands were purposeful.

He did not hesitate. Instinctively he snatched up a statuette that had been curving graciously on a slim pedestal. It went through the glass of the door twice, three times, and then again.

He went through. His right hand was

gashed, and cloth was torn from his shoulder.

As he sprinted away from the entrance, a heavy chair shattered on the ground a few feet away from him. He kept going, weaving as he ran. At any moment there might be shooting. After what he had sensed in there, and after his unavoidable betrayal of what had surged into his mind, there would be no mercy shown to him. If he could be stopped, he would be stopped.

But he made it. He was too far for them — or *it?* — to hold him back now. The monorail station was right ahead.

He didn't hang about, didn't look back. He got the first car headed into the city, and sat in it breathing hard and wondering if his boss would believe the report he was going to hand in.

Superintendent Windsor didn't believe it. He had ribbed Mark Jordan many times before about the troubles of a telepath, but this time he was pompous and admonitory about that eccentric faculty.

'You don't want to get ideas,' he said.

'Your imagination can run away with you just the same as anybody else's — '

'This wasn't imagination. I got it all — quite clear.'

'You're overworked. Reckon I've been pushing you too hard lately.'

'I tell you there's an incredible menace brewing up,' said Mark, desperately. 'This is what we've feared and joked about and argued about for years. The machine that begins to think, to have a personality of its own — and what makes it worse is that it's using the human beings. It's already master of them. I tell you — '

'Your mind's all cluttered up,' said the superintendent, with infuriating sympathy. 'Can't say I blame you. But you don't seriously expect me to . . . well, to call out the riot squad, or try to arrest a house, do you?'

Mark's shoulders slumped. 'No,' he said, wearily. 'I don't expect you to do that. I suppose I don't expect you to do anything. But don't say I didn't warn you.'

Superintendent Windsor suggested a holiday. He was in an unusually amenable mood — but not amenable enough to take action on Mark's daytime nightmare.

'How long,' asked Mark, on a sudden thought, 'before the other houses are ready — the ones on the same design as this?'

'Quit worrying, will you?'

'When?' Mark persisted.

Windsor didn't know and didn't intend to go to the trouble of finding out. Mark had to make enquiries on his own from the Secretary of the Metropolitan Housing Authority. He learned that the building was almost completed and that the lucky tenants would be moving in next week.

He didn't like it. Somebody would have to be made to listen to him, before anything irreparable happened.

Before he could decide who to approach, Windsor insisted that he took a holiday. No arguments. A holiday. 'And get right away from the city and have a good time.'

Mark could not get out of the city. He felt that he must not leave. He was at home ten days later when an urgent message arrived for him from the superintendent.

★ ★ ★

'All right,' said Windsor. 'Let's hear it. Let's hear the whole crazy story, just the way you told it to me.'

Mark glanced quickly round the room, although he was fully awake and his mind had already reached out to make contact as he entered. Someone from the Housing Authority, he noted; Windsor himself and, great heavens, old Morecambe; and a general . . .

'General Sammons,' Windsor was introducing them, 'and this is Mark Jordan, whose report I passed on to you.'

'Yes.' The bright, malicious blue eyes summed him up. 'Well, young feller, let's have it.'

'The house?' said Mark.

'Just that. The house.'

Mark hesitated. But the gravity of their expressions told him that he need hold nothing back. They were not here to pass judgment on him — they had awakened

64

to the menace, something had jarred them into awareness, and it was up to him to tell them just what lay in wait there.

He said: 'That house is alive. It is an entity in itself. You might say lots of houses have a personality, according to the people who live in them. But this is more than that. The men who built that place were too good — they built too well. The brain in that house began to think for itself from the moment it began functioning. Why shouldn't it? Hell, everything was arranged so that it should do just that. How could it *help* thinking for itself?'

'We have had electronic brains for years,' said the man from the Housing Authority stiffly, 'but it has never been suggested that there was any danger of their acquiring a — a personality.'

'Maybe you need human beings to act as . . . well, as batteries,' said Mark. 'I don't know. I haven't worked it out yet. What I do know is that the tenants of that building *belong* to the building. By pooling all their mental resources, the building has made them part of itself. The human beings there are now merely extensions of the sentient creature in which they live.'

The general looked as though he would have liked to snap out something derisive. But he remained silent, tugging at his ginger moustache. It was Morecambe, the Old Man himself, who glared at his subordinate and said:

'Well? And what are we going to do about it?'

'When the people come out of the building,' suggested Mark, 'keep 'em out. Don't let 'em get back in again. It might help. The psychic energy the building has stored up — because that's what it undoubtedly is — will dissipate, or prove powerless without the men and women there.'

Superintendent Windsor pouted like a baby. He said: 'Very nice. But the folks don't come out any more.'

'They have to come out to work,' protested Mark.

'They don't. Not any more. They're just sitting tight.'

'Oh,' said Mark.

'We sent Cartwright in two days ago to investigate a kidnapping — '

'A kidnapping?'

'One of our leading scientists,' interposed the general, allowing himself a gentle sneer at the word that he and his fellow officers always associated with disorder and eccentricity, 'let himself be lured inside by a young technician he knew — feller called Darby — and he just didn't come out again. He was due at an important meeting. Never turned up.'

'We discovered,' Windsor went on, 'that nobody at all was coming out of the place. When we checked up, we found that none of them were turning up at their jobs. Cartwright went in to investigate — and he didn't come out, either.'

'But — '

'We sent a riot squad round there. They couldn't get in. The glass in the doors and windows stood up to their guns — '

'That's something it's learned since I was there,' muttered Mark.

'They couldn't fight their way in,' said Windsor, going red with impotent fury at the memory. 'The place was . . . damn it, it was like a fortress. What the blazes is going on?'

They looked at one another. Then all the rest of them turned and concentrated on Mark. He felt the swirling confusion of their baffled thoughts; and then thrust them out of the way and delved into his memories and impressions of that visit he had made to the great building.

Slowly he said: 'It's getting ready for something. I'm inclined to think it's gathering strength, testing its powers. Learning. You'd better act fast, before it gets really organised.'

The general sat back, jerking upright in his chair. 'Shell the place,' he said.

'No,' cried the man from the Housing Authority. 'Our wonderful new project . . . and, anyway, how wonderful if we can find out just how that brain has come to work like this. If we could get control of it — '

'Get rid of it,' growled the general.

'You've got to get the inhabitants out first,' said Mark. 'Maybe if you can entice them away from the building, the place will lose its psychic potential.'

A wrangle began all about him. Spoken words clashed and conflicted discordantly with the jumble of thoughts and emotions his mind was receiving. He withdrew into cool, analytical contemplation.

'Drop a bomb on it . . . '

'Infiltration . . . '

'Tear gas . . . electronic stunners . . . '

'There'll be hell to pay if we don't get a move on . . . '

Mark said, abruptly: 'Maybe this'll work.'

The clamour was silenced. They looked hopefully at him.

'It had better be good,' said Morecambe, gruffly.

The general nodded and looked ferocious.

Mark said: 'The place isn't yet properly organised. It cannot — how shall I put it? — separate out its various impulses. Or, anyway, that's the impression I've got. When I panicked and turned to run away, there was not much co-ordination in the attempt to stop me. Instead of sending someone out of a side door to intercept me, or getting a really good barrage ready from the upper windows, there was a general rush. The . . . the thing . . . *it* . . . sensed my alarm, got alarmed itself, and flung everything at me just anyhow. Like a kid in a fight, lashing out with arms and legs. No science. But' — his voice became urgent — 'it won't be long before it organises its various limbs, antennae, members — call 'em what you like. The mind of that scientist who was drawn in will teach it a lot. You've got to hit it now, while it's still trying to evolve a *modus vivendi*.'

The general cleared his throat, with the obvious intention of once more advocating immediate annihilation; then he thought better of it, and scowled about him.

Morecambe said: 'How?'

'Do I have to do all the thinking?' protested Mark.

'You're more likely to have a good idea than we are,' said Superintendent Windsor with unaccustomed humility.

Something clicked in Mark's mind. He asked: 'What about the new building — the latest one — are people in it yet?'

'Yes.'

70

'Any — er — developments?'

Windsor said: 'We picked up a messenger on his way from Estate 1 to Estate 2 — '

'Then it has learned to use individuals after all! You didn't tell me that.'

'The chap was pretty clumsy,' said Windsor. 'Walked right into a patrol. He was carrying a manifesto declaring the imminence of a new regime and — I tell you, it was downright screwy — asking for the support of all corporate minds. That's how we got the alarm — why we sent for you.'

'The man himself — what was he like?'

'Vague. Very vague. Like he was in a trance. Still that way last time I saw him.'

'Good. And now then, what about the other house — the occupants of that one haven't barricaded themselves in yet?'

'Not yet.'

'Then get moving. Pick up at least one — preferably more — and let's have them in for treatment.'

'Treatment?'

'I'll explain,' said Mark.

He explained.

Once upon a time, more than a century ago, there had been an unpleasant method of instructing spies in their duties. You kept them awake for days and nights, hammering into their punch-drunk minds a story of their past life. You woke them up just when they thought they were to be allowed a few minutes' sleep, and fired questions at them in the language that was supposed to be their native language. By the time you were finished with them, no torture could have dragged their true identity or the purpose of their mission from them; sometimes they were not even sure of their own original identity. It was an unpleasant process, and it took a long time.

The method applied by Windsor and Mark Jordan was by no means pleasant, but it did not take nearly so long.

The man and two women — he from Estate 1, they from Estate 2, and all three with glazed, unresponsive faces — sat numbly while the pulse generator insinuated its persuasive frequencies into their minds; and as the steady beat stamped down their resistance, Mark was telling them, over and over again, the things that they must believe.

'Estate 2 is a far superior building to Estate 1. It will be the leader. It is more highly developed. You ought to see it. Really, you ought to see it . . . '

Repeated impact, persistent message. When you all go through the doors of Estate 1, you will know that it cannot compare with Estate 2. Really, you ought to see. You ought to see for yourself. No comparison. You ought to see, you ought to see, you really ought to see.

'I've had enough,' Mark said, at last, as dawn came grey into the room.

'You're not the only one.' Windsor wiped his eyes, yawned, and propped his elbows on the table. 'You got me almost believing that stuff. I wonder just how good Estate 2 really is?' He watched morosely as the apparatus was dismantled and the three listless victims led away. 'Do you think,' he asked, 'it'll work?'

'Heaven knows. There were times in the middle of the night when I thought I was insane. Trying to make a block of flats jealous of another block of flats . . . it doesn't make sense.'

'That's what I thought myself,' Windsor frankly agreed.

'But it's got to work. It's got to. If only all the people inside the building will come out —'

'I still don't see why they should.'

Mark sighed. He was beginning to have his own doubts, in the bleak light of morning. But he said doggedly: 'If the impulse is planted there good and strong, it may act impulsively in response. Instinctive jealousy will drive it at once to some sort of action. Maybe we're too late. Maybe it's properly organised by now, and will send just one scout over to report — a scout we won't be able to pick up. But I've got a hunch we may be all right. No organism develops its intelligence right away. Here's a completely new creature — it's got to learn to use what it's got. Even if by some freak a new-born baby was provided with the thinking powers of an adult of twenty-one, I doubt whether it could do much for some weeks or months. Its arms and legs would still wave about, its speech would be confused. It would have to learn . . . and our friend in that building hasn't had any more time to learn than a baby has. Sure, it's got a good mixture of human brains to work on, but my guess is that they're still just that — a mixture. There's a lot of sorting out and classifying and detailing of jobs to be done yet. I hope.'

He went on hoping. There wasn't anything else to be done now.

★　★　★

They were stiff with waiting. It seemed hours since the first guard had been relieved, and yet there were hours until the time came for their own relief.

'Any sign?'

'Not a movement.'

'Quiet, you two along there.'

Stillness again. No lights shone from the building, although the evening was fairly young. It was as though the whole place, sunk in its mental contemplation, building up its mental forces, needed no illumination for ordinary everyday pursuits.

'If this doesn't work,' muttered Windsor to Mark Jordan, 'our friend the general will get his way. They'll have to be starved out.'

'That'll take some time.'

'Superintendent . . .'

There was a sharp whisper. Everybody tensed. Windsor and Mark moved up to the edge of the trees.

'Coming out!'

'How many?'

'Two . . . three . . . four . . . '

Mark held his breath. Dark shapes emerged from the silently opening door, and blended into the shadows. But there were too many of them for the watchers to be in any danger of losing sight of them.

'Give them time to get well away from the place.'

The men were tense and impatient. One false move now and the whole thing might be spoilt. Somewhere a knee-joint creaked, and someone sniggered.

'Now — go get 'em!'

It was almost too easy. The swoop, the rounding-up, the swift retreat from the vicinity of the house. The march away into the lights of the station, and the quick check-up.

None of the tenants would answer questions. They still looked dazed and, surrounded by interrogators, decidedly unhappy. It would take time before they remembered that they were individual human beings again.

'Anybody left inside?' General Sammons was as eager as a terrier, snapping about him, thrusting his head aggressively to right and left.

'According to our check-up, there must be five or six.'

'Probably maintenance staff, or somebody sick,' ventured Windsor.

The general swung on Mark. 'Well? What do we do now? Safe to go in?'

Mark shook his head undecidedly. 'I can't get much out of the minds of these people. It's all a blur — a tangle of emotions and elementary sensations rather than coherent thoughts. But I've got a . . . a feeling there's still a lot of . . . well, call it psychic energy, stored up in there. Feebler than before, perhaps, with only a handful of people there — '

'Fair enough.' General Sammons rapped out orders.

A squad of men with small blast guns moved towards the silent building.

Mark felt fear rising up in his mind as it had risen when he stepped inside those doors. He wanted to call out and stop the men. But his orders would have no effect — they would not stop for him.

A savage burst of firing splintered through the doors, and the men went on in.

There were more shots from inside. Once there was a scream.

'Second squad ready?' said the general grimly.

'Sir' — Mark knew he must speak — 'you must wait until morning.'

'Damnit, young man — '

'You must wait until morning.'

There was such authority in his voice that the general quailed. He went red, and stared at Mark as though he were about to frame a derisive, devastating question. Then he said: 'I suppose you know what you're talking about?'

78

'I'm afraid so,' said Mark.

In the morning they approached the house and trained electronic survey binoculars on the windows. The rooms inside sprang up vividly before their eyes. They saw the men who had gone in, sprawling in their various attitudes: one crushed by a closing door, one strangled by one of the remaining tenants who had kept up the choking pressure even after bullets had been pumped into him, another caught ludicrously and unheroically in the mechanism of a washing machine which had ripped his arms and drained his blood efficiently away . . .

'My God,' whispered the general. Then he stiffened, and swung on Mark. 'I don't care what ideas you've got. I'm going to shell that place. It's still alive.'

'Yes,' said Mark. 'It's got a life of its own now. I'd hoped I was wrong. I'd kept on hoping.'

'It's got to be destroyed. And after it, the other one.'

'Yes.'

They backed away, trying to banish from their minds the nauseating picture of those crumpled bodies. It would always be a nightmare from now on — the metal arms and surfaces, the clutching machines, striking and holding and crushing . . .

'Bring up the guns,' said General Sammons.

The man from the Housing Authority opened his mouth, then looked at their set faces, and closed it again.

★　★　★

Christopher Cardew stood with his wife on the edge of the clearing. In the distance the sound of the train hissing along its monorail was faint and oddly soothing — fainter than the song of birds in the trees or the rustle of the wind in the branches.

He said: 'Well, there it is.'

'We must take it,' she said.

'No labour-saving devices,' he said. 'A generator for electricity, but not much else. Old fashioned electricity,' he added, warningly.

'We'll take it,' she said.

He kissed her, and they walked towards

the sturdy, drab little cottage.

He said: 'You're quite sure?'

'I was wondering . . . '

'Yes?'

'You don't suppose,' she said, 'that we might get hold of some really old stuff — some oil lamps, for example? I'd feel more comfortable.'

4

A habit of hating

Now that I look back and assess it honestly, I've got to admit that I've always felt most intensely alive and somehow more loving when I was hating. Everything's so drab when you're just making polite conversation at a party or listening sympathetically to a friend's problems. Much more fun to be writing blistering letters to British Gas or phoning some cowering little girl on the local council. I've been almost sorry when the stupid little bureaucrats crumble and apologise.

And way back, if one had only had the chance, the guts, all the adult weight and know-how.

School, and all the slights they heaped on you. Dismal daily routine, dismal men who held sway. A schoolmaster plastered with dandruff who once contemptuously kicked my rather shabby satchel out of the way as he strode through the cloakroom. I'd love to go back with my adult powers and ram his face down one of the lavatory pans until he drowned or, even better, choked on his own shit. Yes, I'd still love to do that. And Tubby Blackshaw — a slimy fat bully, always trying to grope your testicles. I dreamed of being bigger and stronger, and twisting his until they came off in my hand.

You think things like that, but of course you don't really mean them, do you?

I did, though. Still do. Still hate the bastards in the past, and find plenty more as time goes by.

Last year a scrawny blonde in the office complained to the Divisional Coordinator that I kept looking at her in a funny sort of way. He laughed when formally questioning me about it. Of course she was a neurotic little drip, and he never for a moment thought that I'd done any such thing.

'I mean, she's hardly worth a second look, eh?'

We laughed, man to man; though he never guessed how much I loathed him, pretentious little brown-noser who'd squelched his way up the promotional ladder.

Of course in this instance he was right. Until then I'd hardly noticed skinny Miss Goffin. Now, although I was careful not to stare too directly, I couldn't help glancing at her in a way that sent her scuttling off down corridors towards offices she hadn't really meant to go to. Having been duly reprimanded, she wouldn't dare risk another complaint. I wondered, in an abstract way, if I could frighten her into throwing herself off the roof, but our labs and offices were a sprawl of single-storey buildings, and even if she could be willed into climbing up on a roof and jumping, she'd probably only thump down on to the grass verges and bruise her bony shoulders.

She was a scrawny little nonentity, but the effect she was having on me proved to be quite stimulating. I was healthily indignant that she should have laid that complaint against me, and found myself ready to spread that hatred over others. Kids who stamped their chewing gum on to pavements: I dreamed of making them scrape it up with their teeth and then swallow it. Women, kids and prams always blocking the pavement while they gossiped below a large clock jutting out from a department store: let it drop on their heads, chiming jubilantly as their screeching voices rasped into silence.

And then there were the things I'd like to inflict on some of my wife's repulsive friends. Just the thought of it . . .

No more than the thought of it, for a while.

To be fair, it wasn't just the office moron or Amanda's friends who were bringing things to the boil. Always simmering away below the surface had been the memory of Deborah's treachery.

Not that I had always hated Deborah. For a long time I neither hated nor loved. I went to bed with honey-haired Deborah in her flat a quarter of a mile from my own bedsitter, stayed the night if it suited me or walked home immediately afterwards if it suited me, along those featureless streets and comfortably into my own bed. That was the way we both wanted it: no commitments, no intensity. Or so I believed. Until she confessed that she was pregnant, and I knew she must have been cheating on me.

Because I'm sterile. Always have been.

That was one of the things that Deborah said suited her just fine, just as it suited me. No risks, no responsibilities. Yet suddenly she was all aglow at the prospect of having a baby.

'I can't expect you to understand, Tony. I really am sorry. Truly I am.'

Truly she wasn't. No way was she sorry. She was bathed in a sickly, self-satisfied radiance. It was a radiance I couldn't share; but I did find some new incitements of my own. Only now, when I knew she had been a shabby cheat all along and I could begin steadily hating her, did those grey streets take on a different light. Instead of drowsing along them, I was wide awake. My mind tingled, I was ready for something. It would show itself soon. Had to be soon. The drizzle glittered a dancing silver, the wet pavements gave off a rich, musky smell. The tatty *Cherry Tree* pub on the

86

corner looked as if it had been newly repainted, and the sound from inside was livelier than it used to be. I swaggered past and thought of Deborah and out loud called her a bitch, and laughed and hated her and laughed all the more. Discarding her and detesting her gave a new shimmering edge to everything else.

Amanda was different.

Different to start with, anyway. I did believe I loved Amanda. We were married and we were happy. Well, content, anyway. We had nothing to quarrel about. I went off each morning to the laboratory, while Amanda went to sit behind the reception desk at a management consultancy, always looking smart and sounding confident in her command of the up-to-the-minute jargon of the trade.

At weekends she devoted herself to our small garden and the greenhouse. We had the neatest possible flowerbeds, and no herb or pot plant could be featured in a colour supplement without it appearing promptly inside or outside the household. Evenings together were tranquil. We played Scrabble a lot, and backgammon. I handed over tips about plant propagation or growth inhibitors which our lab researchers had been testing, and could see her mind wander until she simply had to scurry out to the greenhouse and adjust the heating and do her umpteenth survey of the month. We watched a lot of gardening programmes on the television.

Occasionally we went to bed early, and made love quietly, and slept tranquilly afterwards. Once, after reading a paperback she had been given by one of her firm's clients, she asked me to beat her, which I tried to do lightly and methodically, until something took possession of me and I began to raise weals on her back and she howled and asked me for Christ's sake to stop. But I couldn't. Things between us had been so complacent, so ordinary. Now it was different. She had asked for it, and she was getting it.

Until she struck back. Not physically, but somehow flailing out at me with her mind. My arm was wrenched agonisingly to one side. My fingers went lifeless and I dropped the cane. Sweat broke out on my forehead.

Amanda's voice was a harsh voice I had never heard before. 'You were enjoying that. You liked hurting me.'

'You were the one who wanted it.' I had difficulty in steadying my breathing. 'You asked me to do it.'

'But you enjoyed it so much. Too much.'

She looked at me with a mixture of fear and calculation for a few evenings after that. And something was pulsating inside me, some urgent appetite that had to be satisfied.

It was fed, for starters, by my growing irritation at those silly catchphrases which old school friends consider the height of wit and secret communion.

'Remember the famous occasion when . . . '

'Famous' meaning that nobody outside their own pathetic little clique had ever heard of it or would ever find it in the least amusing.

'And old Miss Murray. The old dragon! Ugh!' Marjorie Johnson, who was married and had two teenage children, still twittered like a gauche teenager herself.

'We believed that at night, in her own room, she paced about breathing flames. One night she'd be bound to set the school on fire with her breath.'

Amanda shuddered with a terror not entirely feigned. She had always had a fear of being burnt alive, trapped in a car or in a room she couldn't get out of.

I wondered what Marjorie's special intimate fear was, and how it could be most poetically and lethally turned against her.

Afterwards, Amanda said: 'Tony, Marjorie was a bit upset, the way you looked at her.'

'What on earth are you on about?'

'She says you gave her a look. Gave her the creeps.'

'The woman does drivel on. Don't any of you ever grow out of those old school hang-ups and bun fights in the dorm?'

And of course there was Bunty with that repulsive dog of hers.

'He's such a great big softie,' she drooled as the hulking great thing slouched about our lawn.

I saw Amanda's face as it crapped on

her wallflowers and then knocked over an urn of fuchsias. 'It doesn't matter,' she said tightly when Bunty apologised as though any apology was an absurdity when the perpetrator of the offence was so lovable. 'Honestly, it doesn't matter a bit.'

But I felt that Amanda wouldn't complain this time if I looked or spoke in a certain way.

'From what I've heard,' I said, 'rottweilers aren't exactly reliable. Likely to turn on their owners without warning.'

'Rubbish.' Bunty sniffed at me just as her dog might sniff before peeing on my leg. 'A lot sweeter tempered than most human beings I know. Much more reliable. And loving.'

I pictured that hefty black and brown beloved turning on her and tearing her apart. Amanda looked at me and went very pale. But we both knew we had an unspoken compact.

A week later in the park, in front of half-a-dozen witnesses — and I'm sorry to say I wasn't one of them — the creature sprang on his besotted owner and sank his teeth into her right arm. By the time it was hauled off, there wasn't much of Bunty's arm that remained user-friendly.

Amanda avoided my eyes when we heard the news, but while I was pouring a drink she said: 'The way you looked at poor Bunty, and at that dog anyone would think you'd wished it on her.'

'You weren't actually wishing her the best of British luck yourself,' I ventured. 'I don't think it could have been done without your collaboration.'

She said nothing. But she knew what I was talking about. And if she was worried, so was I. When the attack happened, I had felt her full power. No matter how she coyly tried denying it to herself, she was the one with the great gift — the true potency for doing what had to be done.

I was envious. She looked so demure and uncomplicated. But she had a gift that, once let loose, I couldn't hope to compete with.

All would be well if we stayed on the same side.

One afternoon I got home to find Amanda already there, earlier than usual, unpacking an emerald dress from a box and laying it reverently on our bed.

'I've been invited out.'

'Some office romance?' I knew it wouldn't be.

'The big boss. Several important clients coming to dinner, and at the last minute he realized they were short of one lady to make up the numbers. Could I step in at short notice — and buy myself a new dress and charge it to the firm.'

'Have a wonderful time,' I said as she left. And I meant it. I didn't begrudge her a treat of this kind, though I hoped she wouldn't move too far, too fast, onto a different level from the one we had comfortably established for ourselves.

On the music centre I was replaying for the fourth time that bit of the concert pieces from Berg's *Lulu* where Lulu is carved up by Jack the Ripper, when the front door opened and Amanda came in, tight-lipped. She had been gone less than an hour.

I flicked the remote control to cut short

the wonderful murderous discords. 'Something wrong? One tycoon refused to sit down with another?'

'The bastard.' Amanda was not crying, but her eyes were blinking furiously. 'The rotten bastard.'

I had never heard her use language like that before, or speak with such venom. Before I could make any soothing noises, or even decide whether they would be welcome, she raged on: 'When I got there, it turned out that one of the men wasn't going to show up, so please I wasn't needed and please would I go home. Only of course the firm would pay for a taxi and I can keep the dress.'

'The bastard.' I said it more quietly than she had done, but much more decisively.

'How can they expect me to go back to that place? How can I be expected to work there, having to see that disgusting swine swaggering in and out every day? I don't think I can bear to be in the same building.'

She collapsed into her usual chair.

'No, I don't see how you can.' I sat

opposite her, both of us in our usual positions. 'He'll have to go, won't he?'

'Don't be silly, Tony. He's the boss.'

'And we have to remove him.'

'You can't be serious?'

I was very serious; and she knew it.

In the morning I phoned the lab to say I would be late, and accompanied my wife to her place of work. We didn't discuss exactly what was going to happen because we didn't know. But we did know, deep down, that something would.

We were there watching, concentrating, when Mr. Broderick's black Merc rolled up and he got out, leaving his chauffeur to ease it round the block to the underground car park entrance. We didn't even know that repairs were going on in the lift shaft. So we could hardly be held responsible, even by ourselves, for the fact that, thirty seconds after the main door had been held open for him by a uniformed commissionaire, Mr. Broderick had somehow stepped into the open shaft just as the lift came down on a test run. Someone had failed to take proper safety precautions.

Or the precautions had been mysteriously overridden.

That evening we silently watched a television programme dealing with the extirpation of garden pests.

The following Tuesday I happened to see Deborah in the street with her little boy wriggling in his pushchair. She was preparing to smile at me, even solicit my congratulations, and I could imagine the twee remarks that would come gushing out. I kept walking straight ahead, and before we drew closer she swung the pushchair perilously across the traffic towards the opposite pavement.

One day she would surely shove it straight under a bus.

Could I make her do that, simply by looking at her? Not that I'd wish any such tragedy on her, of course. It was over long ago, I had nothing to do with her any more, or she with me.

But suddenly the sun was shining, catching the weather vane on the town hall tower, and I laughed, and the day was bright with hatred — honest, invigorating hatred, good for the bloodstream and for striding out . . . and meditating.

One evening Amanda insisted that we throw a dinner party to celebrate the anniversary of two of her group graduating, or one getting married or remarried, or something equally trivial.

'And you won't give them any of your looks, will you?' It was only half a joke.

There were three of her friends — Marjorie, Christine and Penelope — and their husbands: the pimply one, the confident third-level quango administrator who sweated more liberally and grew noisier with each glass of wine, and the weaselly little bank manager. One thing the three men had in common: they all looked sheepish as their wives burbled on about the famous occasion when the loo had overflowed, or the utterly *ghastly* day when that dreadful girl from Shrewsbury had brought not just her dreadful father but his awful floozie blind drunk to prize-giving; and that simply frightful Emma something-or-other who had ruined the school choir's performance of chunks from *Hiawatha* because she couldn't read music but couldn't be chucked out after her father had just presented the school with a new gym.

The women's voices rose half an octave in the squawking ecstasy of reminiscence. I watched their lips twisting, pouting, gushing out banalities, and thought how lovely it would be to petrify each of those faces just as they had reached their most grotesque grimace. Like the old childhood threat about pulling faces just as the wind changed.

As usual, one of them decided it was her turn to dominate the conversation.

This time it was Penelope Bibby, whose husband was the quangocrat. On a basis of nudge-nudge secrets which he had confided to her, she liked to do her own bit of nodding and winking, keen to air her knowledge about the workings of insurance companies and investment analysts being given a hard time by a Sunday business supplement investigation.

'I mean, I ask you, some of the things these companies bury in the small print! I mean, look at *our* policy. Do you have a smoke alarm, do you have a fire escape, do you smoke in bed, do you make love at too high a temperature?' She sniggered. 'I suppose you meet all the right criteria, Amanda? Still got the rope ladder? Always had it,' she confided to the rest of us, 'in the dorm. Scared stiff of being burnt alive. Not that they ever pampered us with a proper fire. But Amanda insisted on keeping her rope ladder coiled up under the bed.'

Amanda had gone very pink and wasn't laughing. I knew it was true, but it wasn't one of the memories she liked to toss to and fro. I tried to turn it against the others by asking what each of them was most scared of.

All the women started babbling at once, as if proud of their lovable little fears and failings. Penelope, anxious to cover up her gaffe, was the loudest of all in her eagerness to tell us of her nightmare of a car windscreen shattering in her face while driving. 'Broken glass,' she wailed. 'My eyes, I'm so sensitive about my eyes. Can't even bear to have a doctor examining them.'

Tom Bibby said: 'Modern windscreens don't shatter like that.' The weariness in his tone made it obvious that he had told her this a dozen times before.

Christine admitted to a terror of moths and butterflies. Her husband looked embarrassed. I said breezily that he ought to take her to the butterfly farm ten miles away and shake her out of it.

Christine shuddered and glared at me.

Penelope challenged me: 'And what about you, Tony? What scares the pants off you?'

'Women,' I said. 'Only it's not so much a matter of scaring them off me . . . '

Penelope made a face, but the others laughed thinly, and the moments of tension were over. For the time being.

When Amanda went out to the kitchen to bring on a fruit pudding she had slaved over after reading the recipe in the back of her gardening magazine, I took some plates out to clear the table. I kissed her. She looked startled. We didn't usually get demonstrative out of bed, but I felt something reaching between us, coming to fulfilment. I welcomed the sensation; but she was trying to keep it at arm's length.

Clasping her hands round the fruit bowl as if to steady herself, she said: 'I suppose Penny really is getting a bit of a bore.'

We went back in. Neither of us looked at Penelope, who was still rattling on.

Tom Bibby was uneasy. I could tell he wanted his wife to shut up, but he wasn't going to say so in front of the rest of us.

That night Amanda and I made love more fiercely than either of us had been used to. When it was over, she panted: 'You were thinking of Penny.'

'Penelope? Good God, I've never fancied — '

'Not fancying her, I mean, you're thinking of how to . . . wipe her out. And I don't want anything to do with it.'

'You're sure of that?'

'Of course I'm sure.'

My arm was around her damp shoulders, my lips close to her left ear. 'If you don't want to, it won't work. And it already is working, just the way it did with your boss.'

'That was an accident.'

'One that you willed.'

She was trembling in the darkness, only it wasn't really dark. The bedroom was filled with a wonderful light. 'Tony, what's going to happen?'

'We'll have to wait and see.'

The trouble was that we didn't actually see it. All we got were garbled but colourful reports a week later.

Tom and Penelope had been at home, having a candle-lit dinner. Very romantic, I'm sure. They didn't notice one of the candles burning down faster than the other, until the glass candlestick cracked. Slivers of glass exploded into Penelope's face, one of them long enough and sharp enough to reach her brain.

And I wasn't even there to see it.

At the funeral we all shook hands in a silly, solemn way. The women had taken the opportunity to look very chic in their sadness. Christine was wearing a fine black veil. 'Charming,' I said. 'Just like a butterfly net.'

If she could have spat at me through the veil, I think she'd have done so.

Her husband was at my elbow. 'Haven't you done enough damage?' He snapped out that he had been stupid enough to listen to me, and had taken her to the butterfly farm. 'She's starting treatment with a psychiatrist. Going to cost me a bloody fortune.'

It was funny. Of course it had to be funny. There's no pleasure in creating horror for anybody else if you're horrified yourself. It has to be a superb joke, so private and overwhelming that you don't want to share it with anybody else.

Except with a partner who can contribute.

Late at night, in bed holding hands while Amanda kept sobbing, 'No . . . no, please no, Tony,' as if I were raping her, we found ourselves concentrating on Christine. In spite of all the girlish matiness, between them there must be old scores to settle from way, way back. So together we flooded Christine's mind with a whirl and swirl of butterflies, and when she screamed and reached out to turn the light on, we willed a squadron of moths towards the bulb.

Two days later we heard that Christine had gone away for 'a rest cure', as

Marjorie half fearfully, half gloatingly put it,

'Tony, that's enough.' Amanda flinched when I put my hand on her arm. 'It's got to stop. We're pushing them into things they're terrified of.'

'More fools them.'

One Saturday afternoon we went out for a walk. If we hadn't been together, our minds not concentrating on anything in particular, but free to interlock if triggered, things might not have worked out as they did.

On the slope above the supermarket we saw Deborah pushing her little boy uphill in his pushchair with a load of groceries in the basket. She glanced at me and looked away.

Amanda said: 'Isn't that the girl you used to . . . I mean, before we . . . '

'Yes, that's her.'

'What right has she got to have a child?'

It was the first time Amanda had ever mentioned the matter. I couldn't be sure whether it was her own resentment, or something she had telepathically picked up from me. But we both felt the tug of it, the sudden fierce brightness all round us, and something almost like a halo enfolding the pushchair.

It broke away from Deborah's grip and began running downhill, gathering speed. There was nobody close enough to stop it plunging under an artic swinging towards the delivery bay of the supermarket. Somebody somewhere began screaming. And beside me, Amanda was sobbing, 'No, I didn't mean it, I didn't, didn't . . . '

It made quite a mess, as if tins of tomatoes in the load had burst and spilt their squashed red contents into the gutter.

I tried to put an arm round Amanda, but she wrenched herself away. 'How could you make me do that?'

'I didn't make you do anything you didn't want to.'

Our evenings were no longer so tranquil. At the appointed hour we tried to turn our minds to backgammon or Scrabble, but one evening when she came up with the word MURDER she tried to make out that I had somehow controlled the order of letters. She must have known that it was her own fingers that had selected them. We didn't go on with that game or ever start another one.

We weren't invited to meals with those of her friends who remained, and we didn't invite them to our home any more.

Looking at Amanda across the fireplace one evening, I had a chill feeling that all the joy of hating outwards had been turned inwards. Things I had detested in her friends were deeply ingrained in her, too. How could I ever have married a girl called Amanda? It was such a stupid name. I must always have hated the name Amanda without facing up to the fact. Now it grew daily more and more hateful. Her mannerisms were not just as bad as those of her nauseating clique, but worse. I had never noticed before that when we tried to sit quietly reading, she had a habit of lifting a page long before she was ready to turn it over, and scratching the inner edge with a fingernail. And when at last I could bear it no longer and was taking a deep breath before complaining, she said, without looking up: 'Do you have to keep clicking your tongue against your teeth like that?'

It dawned on me, almost too late, not only that I hated her and could now feel free to hate her, but that she felt the same about me.

Who was going to make the first move?

One Saturday evening I half closed my eyes and willed her to lean forward and fall towards the fire. Like all the others, a straightforward accident, But nothing happened. When she glanced up, I could see in her eyes that she sensed what had been in my mind. Her defences were primed.

There was a high wind that night. I heard slates fall on the dustbin and the path beside the back door. On the Sunday morning, Amanda tried to persuade me to fetch a ladder and see to the slates. I said I preferred to wait until Monday and get someone in who was properly qualified for that kind of work.

'You're scared,' she said.

'I've got no head for heights. You know that.'

Yes, she knew, all right. But although

she concentrated on me, there was no way that on her own she could will me up on to that roof. She was stronger than I, and I was growing to envy that and to hate her all the more — all her pretences of unwillingness, of being led astray by me — but never quite strong enough if I resisted. Her only chance was if she could catch me unawares.

And the same went for me and my chances.

I worked a lot of overtime in the lab, doing simple jobs that required no concentration. Every day was bright now with promise. All the lab equipment shone as if newly installed and not yet stained by use. My mind shone implacably. I was truly alive, made doubly alert by fear and my own power to inflict fear.

I couldn't destroy Amanda in anything like the way the others had been destroyed. No remote control this time, and certainly not powerful back-up from her. It had to be close and real. I had to be right there on the spot. This time I wanted to *see* it happen.

On the afternoon when I finally made

up my mind, I stayed a long time in the *Cherry Tree* on the way home. I pretended to have had more to drink than I'd really had, blundering into the umbrella stand on the way in and chucking a batch of pages torn from a technical magazine on to the coffee table, grunting as if I had a hard evening's work ahead of me.

She hardly bothered to listen to me. She had been turning over the pages of a glossy gardening magazine, scratching each page as she did so. Even if I'd had any doubts, that would have settled it. When she went out to talk gibberish to some seedlings in the greenhouse, I waited a few moments and then followed her.

She was always relaxed in those surroundings. Too relaxed. When she saw me coming, it was too late.

I swear I didn't actually make it happen. Not physically. It was just that I looked at the gas cylinder connected to the greenhouse heater, and as I looked, it suddenly vomited flame. I was nowhere near it, honestly. But all at once the whole greenhouse was a vast glass oven. Amanda was engulfed in flame as she screamed and groped towards the door.

The only thing I actually did was turn the key outside, and then when the smell of burnt flesh was billowing through the cracks in the blistered glass, turned it back again. Then I went indoors and called the ambulance.

There was no way her rope ladder was going to get her out of that.

At the funeral, those of her friends still alive stared at me. I didn't know all of them, but somebody seemed to have passed on tales about me. None of the women went in for the usual slobbering kisses, and their husbands didn't shake my hand.

As I walked away from the graveside, I looked up at the top of the church tower. Even craning my neck at this angle made me dizzy. That must have been why I saw Amanda so clearly up there, willing me to come and join her at the parapet. And there were other shapes crowding in behind her, and some behind me and around me. A wisp of Penelope, a long wail from Marjorie. All of them urging me to go into the stair turret and climb to the top. But there was no reason to be scared of shadows, even shadows who knew from what had been said at those dinner parties, or hinted at by Amanda during one of their hen parties, about my fear of heights. What remained of Amanda wasn't strong enough on her own to drag me up there, and those other wraiths were as pathetic dead as when they had been alive.

My feet firmly on solid ground, all I'm conscious of is this emptiness now it's all over. Now Amanda's dead, I'm looking impersonally at what I've done, yet at the same time looking at it in dismay. Because I've destroyed the only person who could have shared the joke.

Like I said, loving and hating are so close. I'd loved Amanda. Really loved her, in my own way. It was her own fault that she'd had to be killed, and the true horror is that now there's nobody left to love or hate.

Except myself.

And I don't hate myself. Well, not all that much. Not yet.

And when I do . . . ?

5

Stand-in

It was not until the middle of the evening that she began to have her suspicions. Walter had been so assiduously attentive that she had instinctively relaxed, soothed by his affectionate voice and his still-youthful smile. It was not until she yawned and suggested they should go to bed early that she sensed something was wrong. He looked ever so slightly disconcerted. Then he said, brightly: 'It's a bit early yet.'

She studied him for a moment. 'Is there anything wrong, dear?'

'Not at all,' he said.

'It would do us good to make an early night of it. We'll have a nice drink first.'

She flicked the switch near her chair, and sat back in the comfortable anticipation of being shortly presented with hot chocolate from the service chute.

Walter, rather too airily, said: 'I don't

really feel tired yet. I think I'll sit up a little bit longer.' He paused, as though considering his own remark judicially, and then added: 'But you run along, darling. As soon as we've had our drink, you run along.'

She looked away, feeling more than ever uneasy. It just couldn't be — he would surely never have done such a thing . . . ? It couldn't be. She wouldn't let herself believe it.

But once the idea was in her mind, she couldn't just pretend that it wasn't there. There was only one way of finding out.

Casually she got up and walked across the room. A quick glance at the door of the wine cupboard showed that Walter's panel was locked. She opened the drawer to get the emergency key — and discovered that it was not there.

She drew a deep breath and turned to face the inquiring gaze of her husband.

She said: 'Walter, I know what you are. You're not yourself.'

'Really, darling . . . '

The reply was feeble and uncertain. It quite decided her. *They* could never grapple with a really awkward situation.

Walter was getting up. She glanced quickly round the room, and saw the old-fashioned poker that Walter insisted on having in the ornamental fireplace — for all his technical brilliance and belief in progress, Walter had a great longing for old traditions, and a rather naive affection for old-world charm in his home. She was glad of it now. She grabbed the poker, brushed past Walter, and drove the end of the poker through the woodwork of the wine cupboard.

'No!' cried Walter.

She twisted the metal against the lock, and a moment later the door cracked open, showering jagged splinters and fragments on to the floor.

Then she reached in and cut off the control switch inside the shattered panel.

She turned round once more and said: 'Well?'

There was no reply. She had known there would not be any. Walter stood in the middle of the room, staring in front of him, motionless. His mildly protesting expression had frozen on his features and made him look puzzled and absurd. He did not speak.

Barbara said a rude word, knowing that the lifeless figure before her would not hear it.

The delivery chute clicked a warning and delivered two beautifully steaming cups of hot chocolate. Barbara sat down and drank both of them. Then she got up and walked round Walter to mix herself a cocktail — a fiery one.

She put the light out and sat in the darkness, waiting — waiting and fuming, stung by resentment.

How could he do this to her? How could he, how could he . . . ?

She had to wait for half an hour, though it seemed more like several hours. At last she heard cautious movements near the back door. She kept silent until footsteps approached the door of the room in which she was sitting, and then she said, 'All right, you can come in.'

There was a pause.

'Come along in,' she said, angrily. 'It's no good hanging about out there.'

The door opened, and Walter came in.

He switched on the light, and looked sheepishly at himself standing in the middle of the room. Barbara said: 'Aren't you going to say anything? Don't just goggle at me like a . . . a robot.'

'I suppose it's hard for you to understand,' he said, tentatively.

'Hard?' She exploded from her chair, almost launching herself at him as though she intended to knock him over. 'It's certainly not easy to understand why a man should sneak off out without explaining to his wife where he's going, and leaving a robot to entertain her. I never thought you could do such a thing to me.'

They were both standing close to the silent version of Walter. His presence irritated both of them at the same moment. Barbara said, ridiculously: 'Oh, do go away.' And her husband went to the cupboard and switched on.

His other self rocked slightly, then blinked and looked self-consciously at Walter.

'Good evening, sir. You're back early.'

'I am not back early,' said Walter,

frostily. 'I am back at the time I arranged — and what do I find? I find you asleep on the job.'

'I fear that Mrs. Desmond must have switched me off.'

'Well, just go and stow yourself away for the night,' said Walter vindictively, 'and I'll switch you off again.'

He watched the robot walk gracefully across the room and out into the hall. There was a gentle click as the door of the storage closet snapped shut. Walter switched off.

'Well?' said Barbara, quietly. She was still waiting. 'I think you owe me an explanation.'

'It was a matter of business, dear . . . '

'Funny business,' said Barbara.

'Please don't be crude about it, darling. It was just that I had to go to this conference, and after what you'd said about us never having an evening at home together nowadays, I felt you wouldn't be too pleased.'

'But the whole point of having those robots made,' protested Barbara, 'was to enable us to stay at home. It's him,' she went on, with ungrammatical fervour, 'who ought to have gone to your precious conference. That's what he's for.'

'But this was rather a special one. I needed to make decisions — important ones concerning future policy on robot construction for the Government. I simply had to be there. It wasn't just a routine matter that I could leave to Wally.'

Barbara pouted. She was not going to be soothed. She said: 'But even if it's true — and I'm not sure it is — even if it's time, how could you leave Wally with me like that? To leave a robot to entertain your wife . . . that's too much, Walter.'

'I didn't want you to be upset.'

'You didn't want me to be upset? Suppose you hadn't come home — suppose you'd left it with me all night, would it . . . that is, how far were you prepared for it to . . . er . . . '

'Barbara!' Walter was indignant. 'Nothing like that could have happened. In any case, there was no question of my not getting back. I had set it to nip out into the garden when I brought the gravicop down into the garage. When I got back

118

and Wally didn't appear, I guessed something has gone wrong.'

'I still don't see why you had to play such a trick on me. I don't see why you couldn't have sent Wally to the meeting.'

He sighed. 'I've told you. We had to make decisions about new developments. The Government's check on robot construction is hopelessly out of date, and we want to let some of the higher-ups know just what possibilities there are — we want a freer hand in design and so on.'

'It'll spoil things if everyone has robots like ours.'

'I don't mean to go that far. The authorities would have a fit if they knew we'd been able to produce humanoids like this. They still won't give permission for anything but the most obviously mechanical, box-like contrivances. That's what we want to get cleared up. That's why I had to go to this meeting tonight and discuss future policy, and what weight we could bring to bear on the Government. And I knew you'd been counting on us having a nice quiet evening

together, so . . . ' He shrugged apologetically.

Barbara tried to continue with her
resentful expression, but her original
anger was fading.

She said: 'Oh, all right. But don't think
I'm not cross. And this had better be the
last time.'

'It will be, darling.'

'Mind it is.'

'Of course. It won't happen again.'

She studied him reflectively. 'It *is* the
first time, this one, I suppose? You haven't
ever done it before?'

'You'd have noticed,' said Walter, glibly,
'just as you noticed this time. I ought to
have known I couldn't fool you with
Wally.'

'No, that's true,' said Barbara. 'But
— you're quite sure you haven't ever . . . ?'

'Quite sure,' lied Walter.

*   *   *

Walter loved his wife. There was no doubt
about that. In his own way he loved her as
devotedly as she loved him; but his way

was not quite as demonstrative as hers. There were times when her intensity proved just a little bit overpowering — Walter found it hard to keep pace with her eager chatter; he knew that his inability to cope with her affectionate and effusiveness often made it seem that he was cold and unresponsive. And that wasn't true. But it was true that he liked, now and then, to get away and have a breathing space. He found an evening meeting of his colleagues at the research centre a relaxation, rather than an arduous duty.

He was sorry that Barbara had detected Wally this time. The robot had served a similar purpose two or three times before, and Walter had thought that all was now well. But even the most convincing humanoid developments — and Wally was one of the finest models they had ever created — could not be entirely reliable. He would have to be careful in future. Barbara could be quite exhausting when she really lost her temper, and Walter was all in favour of a quiet life. It was, in fact, his desire to make life less arduous that had resulted in the construction of Wally, and Wally's companion model, Babs.

The Robot Research Foundation, and its associated manufacturing and exploiting companies, had been brought into being by Walter's father. Working under Government supervision because of the alarm that was felt in certain quarters about the development of pseudo-intelligent beings, the Foundation had produced robots for every conceivable purpose.

From the humblest of new labour-saving devices to the most complicated electronic brains, R.R.F. had a virtual monopoly of the field. Smooth-running mechanical servants were provided. Robot traffic controllers were installed in all the major cities, and robots took over many police duties. No warehouse needed to employ a human watchman; no monorail express needed a driver; no restaurant required the services of more than two or three human beings to keep cooking and waiting up to the highest possible standard.

But there were stringent regulations. Strides in robot manufacture had been so enormous in twenty years that a great many people felt uneasy. Religious bodies in particular voiced energetic protests about the construction of humanoid beings — mechanical creatures so life-like that they could be mistaken for human beings. Laws were passed forbidding the construction of such highly advanced models. A machine was to be kept recognisably a machine. The grafting of skin and the introduction of natural mobility were forbidden.

Wally and Babs were very special . . . and their existence was undoubtedly a breach of the law.

'Wouldn't it be wonderful,' Barbara had once said to her husband, 'if there could be two of each of us, so that when there was some boring party on, we could send our other selves along. And when you had some silly old meeting, you could let your Number Two trot along, while you stayed at home with me.'

'Mm,' was all that Walter had said; but the remark fermented in his mind, and before long a few of his most trusted workmen began to experiment with a new hush-hush design.

When they were finished, Wally and Babs looked perfect — as perfect, that is, as one would expect a normal human being to look. In deportment they were graceful, and their conversation was flawless. Their electronic minds, stored with appropriate memories, and fed from time to time with such information as their owners thought they ought to possess, coped neatly and efficiently with any question that was put to them. From a basis of known facts and routine data they could extrapolate in a way that even Walter Desmond had to admire — their conversation was much smoother and far less grudging than his own tended to be. Indeed, there were times when he found himself looking with some affection at Babs. Babs was always more affable and less argumentative than Barbara. He could talk to Babs — in fact, he had once or twice caught himself talking the most utter nonsense to Babs, and receiving neatly phrased, unembarrassed replies that eventually brought him to his senses.

They were a useful pair. No one would

have suspected their essential unreality — no one, that is, who didn't know of their existence — and there were very few people who did, and they could all be trusted to keep the secret.

It was a pity, thought Walter again, that his wife had guessed that she had been fobbed off with the substitute for an evening. Next time he must try to ensure that she couldn't get at the switch — it made him wince when he looked at the shattered horror of that beautiful cupboard door.

Next time . . .

★   ★   ★

As it happened, the next occasion on which he planned to go out with the boys for a pleasant evening gave him the chance of an interesting experiment.

'You haven't forgotten that Simon is coming in tonight, have you, darling?' said Barbara.

In point of fact he had completely forgotten, but he said: 'No, of course not.' Then he thought about it for a moment, and added: 'Though I don't see why he keeps hanging around.'

'Don't you, darling?'

That exaggerated archness of hers annoyed him intensely. It was so stupid. There was no question of his being jealous of Simon — after all, Simon hadn't married Barbara, and he himself had, and that was that. But it irritated him to see the silly idiot posturing and hovering around Barbara, saying meaning, ironical things that he thought Walter was too dense to understand. And although Barbara agreed that Simon was an utter fool, she did seem to get a kick out of that sort of pretentious nonsense.

He said: 'It's time Simon grew up and found himself a wife.'

'I'm afraid he has lost the only ideal woman in his life,' Barbara said smugly.

'Well, a fat lot of good it'll do him to brood over it,' said Walter.

It was not until later in the day that he realized what an opportunity was being offered to him. He wanted to go out and play a game of Martian slides with a few of the boys, and this time it would surely be safe to let Wally take over at home. Barbara was always too busy mopping up Simon's florid compliments and simpering at his jokes to pay much attention to her husband. Walter could have a couple of hours out and then return, work an unobtrusive switch with Wally, and take over in time to usher Simon out of the house and silently wish him good riddance.

There was hardly any risk to it at all. He slipped out that evening full of confidence.

And Wally strolled back into the room Walter had just left, accepted a drink from the cocktail mixer, and smiled placidly at Simon.

It was the placidity of that smile that eventually aroused Barbara's suspicions.

She had been listening to Simon for almost an hour, and thinking how very sweet he was. It was all very well for Walter to sneer and say how damned silly and futile all that gush was — Walter was an undemonstrative type, and not much given to the paying of pretty compliments; but that didn't mean that there was anything wrong with the paying of compliments. Walter just didn't understand how a woman appreciated such things. A woman liked to be flattered and made a fuss of. She liked to be complimented delicately on her appearance; and how could you resist the yearning in the eyes of a man who obviously still loved you and longed for you?

There were even moments — she shivered at the disloyal thought, but it was rather a delicious shiver — when she wished she had married Simon instead of Walter.

No, perhaps that wasn't altogether true. But it would be nice to have a little affair with Simon. Nothing too serious, of course. As long as she still loved Walter, you couldn't say she was really being unfaithful. Not really.

She blushed and looked down at her hands, folded demurely in her lap.

Simon came and curled up at her feet. He was too adorable. He could do a thing like that without looking in the least self-conscious or awkward.

He murmured: 'Come out with me

tomorrow evening.'

'Oh, I don't know . . . I mean . . . '

'Walter won't mind,' said Simon in a louder voice. 'After all, he doesn't appreciate you as he ought to. I've always said you don't appreciate her, haven't I, Walter?'

'Yes,' said Walter, placidly.

'And you don't mind if I got out with Simon for the evening?' asked Barbara, staring at him.

He smiled at her. 'I shall be torn apart with jealousy,' he said with a smooth gallantry that struck a chill to her heart, 'but I know that right will triumph in the end. I shall be waiting for you when you return, sobbing and disillusioned.'

Even Simon looked mildly surprised. But he said: 'I rejoice to hear it, old man.'

Barbara looked away. She was afraid that her expression would betray her. At the first opportunity she stole a glance at the cupboard. It had been repaired on the broken side, and both panels were now locked. And even if she could have got at it, she would not have dared to switch off with Simon here. If her suspicions were right and this was Wally in the room with them, she could not switch him off — she could not let the garrulous Simon into the secret.

Nevertheless, she felt an impulse to do so, to put an end to the whole thing, to show Walter up for the deceitful, wretched rogue he was. It was an impulse that she restrained.

But she would show him. Somehow or other, she would get her own back on him.

She went out into the hall. The door of Wally's storage closet was locked. She opened the door of the compartment in which Babs stood, motionless, and studied her thoughtfully. Then she went back to join the men — or, rather, the man and the shadow — and said brightly to Simon:

'I really think it would be nice to come out with you, Simon.'

And the false face of Walter smiled without the trace of a sneer.

★   ★   ★

When Walter himself returned, he changed places with Wally in the garden.

'Anything special I ought to know?' he asked.

'Mrs. Desmond has accepted an invitation to go out with Mr. Collings tomorrow evening,' Wally reported.

'Has she? Good heavens, she must be potty.'

Wally was too innately respectful to pass any judgment on this remark.

'All right,' said Walter, as they approached the house. 'Wait until I'm well inside, and then stow yourself away. It may be ten minutes or so before I get an opportunity of switching you off, so don't start fidgeting about.'

Then he strolled nonchalantly indoors and joined his wife and Simon. 'Another drink?' he said.

'Not for me, old boy. It's time I was running along.'

Walter did not press Simon to stay. He waited until Barbara had finished fussing over him at the front door, and then, as she was plumping up the cushions and whisking about the room in her usual erratic way, he said: 'I suppose you're serious about going out with Simon tomorrow?'

'Of course, darling. You don't mind?'

'I don't mind,' he said. 'I just can't imagine why you should want to spend an evening with that absurd bore. One evening of flattery ought to be enough for anyone.'

She laughed. 'Yes, I don't know that I really want another dose of Simon's conversation. It's so meaningless, isn't it? If only it led to something — '

'To what?' said Walter, aggressively.

'Well, if there were any purpose in it . . . you know what I mean . . . but in the nature of things it can't lead up to anything, can it? After all, I'm married to you, and Simon's too late.'

'I should think so. I can't understand why you should take such pleasure in leading him on.'

Barbara said, abruptly: 'Don't you want me to go, darling?'

'As we've had Simon's company all evening, I thought we might have a quiet time together tomorrow.'

'How sweet of you, darling. Perhaps you're even a little bit jealous?'

'Jealous be damned,' snorted Walter. 'I know you've got too much sense to care a damn for anyone as thick-headed as Simon — '

'He's not all that thick-headed. He says nice things to me.'

'Oh, all that bosh . . . '

She looked at him with her candid, thoughtful grey eyes. Then she said, softly: 'You're far too arrogant, Walter. But there's nothing I can do about that now, is there? If you order me to stay in tomorrow evening, I'll have to do as I'm told.'

'Nonsense. If you want to go out with Simon, you go out.'

'I could send Babs,' she said, with the flicker of a smile.

The smile struck echoes. Walter began to laugh. It was really an awfully good idea. Simon would be far too dense to notice the difference — Simon would be delighted by the gentleness and politeness of the duplicate Barbara.

He said: 'That's splendid. That's really

wonderful. He'll never know. Even when he kisses her he won't notice the difference.'

'What makes you suppose I allow Simon to kiss me?'

'Oh, a friendly peck now and then . . . it doesn't mean anything. No need to be worried about it,' Walter went on, chuckling. 'Poor Simon!'

'Poor Simon,' echoed Barbara.

The thought of the hoax kept on recurring to Walter during the course of the following evening. He had watched Barbara dressing Babs ready for the evening out, and when, just before Babs left, the two of them came into the room in a flurry of womanish excitement, Babs was so convincing and so very human that he gave her a drink with an instinctively courteous bow of appreciation.

'Old Simon's going to have a wonderful time,' he jeered when he and Barbara were alone together. 'Damn it, he's a very lucky chap. Not everyone has such excellent substitutes provided.'

'Simon is very lucky,' Barbara agreed.

Barbara was very sweet and agreeable all evening. She was a little quieter than usual, as though perhaps regretting the trick she was playing on Simon. But when Walter made a joke about the situation and said, not for the first time, 'Poor Simon,' she smiled and echoed his words. He began to feel that he ought to give up his rather risky ventures away from home in the evenings. It was much more pleasant to sit here and talk to his wife, from time to time switching on the visio and watching the soothing colours and images on the far wall. Music throbbed gently through the room. He drowsed.

Barbara did nothing to disturb him. It was Walter himself who was the first to notice how late it was getting. He thrust himself up from his chair and said: 'Where's Babs got to?'

Barbara shrugged. 'She can't come to any harm.'

'No, but . . . confound it all, it's two in the morning. And Simon doesn't know that Babs is Babs. If he thinks he's out with you, he has no business to be out until this hour. It's a disgrace.'

'Everything will be all right,' said Barbara placidly.

'You're talking it all very calmly. I mean, I should have thought you'd be insulted — '

'No,' she said, 'not insulted.'

Although the room glowed with mellow light, the feeling of night had descended. Outside would be darkness. It was high time Babs was home. Walter felt rather like an indignant father waiting for an errant daughter. He was surprised that Barbara should be so unconcerned.

He reached a sudden decision. He said: 'Give me the key for your cupboard.'

'The key?'

'Yes. I'll switch off Babs. That'll give Simon a shock.'

'But you can't do that. He'll raise an awful fuss. And then everyone will find him out, and — '

'We'll give him a few minutes to get in a panic, then I'll call him on the visiscreen and tell him what's happened. He deserves a shock. Fancying his chances with my wife — or with what he thinks is my wife!'

Barbara shook her head, but seemed unable to speak

'The key, darling,' said Walter, impatiently.

She took it from her pocket and held it out reluctantly. He turned to the cupboard and opened the panel.

'The way you take it so calmly,' he said, as he reached for the switch, 'anyone would think you were Babs. Now, that would be funny — if you were Babs and I was Wally and we were sitting here talking while all the time our real selves were out somewhere . . . You know, I've almost got myself wondering if I am the real one, after all.'

He turned, laughing.

There was no reply. Barbara sat staring in front of her. She did not move, did not speak.

Walter said in a hushed, strained voice: 'No. No.'

He went over and touched her. She did not respond. The finger of the clock moved smoothly and remorselessly on.

'Oh, no,' said Walter again.

He sat down heavily in the chair facing

the immobile Babs. He sat there waiting, staring as though hypnotized at the calm, beautiful face before him — staring, and remembering the living face that this one imitated.

And at last, painfully, he began to understand the meaning of jealousy.

6

Acute Rehab

At first, in a dreamlike way, it was funny. Each time a nurse asked him for his date of birth before giving him pills or an injection, he was tempted to say, 'I haven't a clue,' or, 'I wasn't there at the time.' And anyway, since the date was clearly printed on the plastic bracelet round his wrist, why did they have to keep asking?

'To be sure it's the right patient,' one nurse condescended at last. 'We must be sure not to give the wrong treatment to the . . . the case in hand.'

She had attractively oval features, but her cheeks were very pale, almost transparent, and her eyes were remote, as if waiting for orders. Nurses, of course, were probably always tense, waiting for orders or primed to act in an emergency; but he had never expected one to be so . . . well, out of reach, too far away to bother with him calling out if he needed her.

She receded into a haze. The after-effects of the anaesthetic came swamping over him yet again, stirred into a slow whirlpool by the addition of painkillers and God knows what else they had stuffed into him.

The surgeon was there, smiling, looking satisfied, yet had nothing reassuring to say.

From out of the haze, the repetitive chant: 'What's your date of birth?'

He was propped up, given food and a little pot of multi-coloured pills; and then it was night, and then another morning.

'What's your date of birth? We do have to be sure we've got the right treatment for the right person.'

'Look, when do I get out of here? All right, I ran over a bloke and I'll have to face up to that in court. But — '

'You killed him.'

'It was an accident.'

'So you say.'

'I suppose I'm under special supervision here?'

'You could say that.'

Another day. Dull. Repeated. 'Your date of birth?'

'Oh, for Christ's sake — '

'A bit late to call on that name. After your sin against that child, ten years old, ten years ago. And the way you neglected your wife and — '

'No, that's rubbish. Where did you get all that crap?'

'People talk under anaesthetic. And under sedation. And we do have our records. This is where we collect and assess such things. And decide.'

'Decide what?'

It came again, a drone of a voice without interest or the hint of a friendly laugh at the boring absurdity of it. 'Your date of birth?'

'Look,' he asked again, 'when do I get out of here? I suppose I'll have to go to court and face up to dangerous driving and hitting that young man — '

'Killing him. The surgeon's son.'

'What?'

No, there were so many disjointed things jumbling together in his mind, so many shadows and sudden stabs of

141

colour, a buzzing of voices and sounds that were nothing like voices . . .

How did they know that he had known all along that it was the surgeon's son?

There in front of him as he was driving past the hospital. The cocky young bastard. One of the youngest surgeons ever, was the boast. In fact the swaggering little sod had got there only because his father had been who he was. Pulled out every stop for him.

He hadn't set out to kill the bastard. It was just that . . . well, there he was, right in front of the car, too damn conceited to bother looking where he was going.

Time to brake and shout at the arrogant little sod?

Maybe.

But actually I put my foot down, didn't I, and went straight at the man, the young so-called consultant whose negligence had caused my wife's death, for which I was blamed on grounds of neglect but for which he was completely exonerated. And after the impact the car was suddenly skidding and hit the lamp standard and I was over on my side . . .

His side. A physical awareness crept through the trauma of post-operative fantasies. He tried to turn over on his right side. But there was something missing from that side, making it awkward. Making it impossible.

'Nurse!' It was little more than a croak.

'Lie still, now. Don't fuss, it'll only make it worse.'

'My right leg. What's happened to — '

'It had to come off. To free you from your car. Mr. Halliburton himself — '

'Halliburton? But he's the one I hit, he was jaywalking and — '

'Mr. Halliburton senior.'

'You don't mean — you can't mean — they let his old man saw my leg off? Bloody hell, that's unethical. He had no right — '

'In an emergency, he acted for the best. Here, we all act for the best.'

Another day, lying here.

Another day, exactly the same.

Boring.

The son's clumsiness destroyed my

wife, and now his father has begun destroying me.

Thoughts stifling. Nightmares on and on . . . punishing . . .

'Your date of birth?'

Another day, just the same, devoid of meaning, with yet another one to come tomorrow . . . how many more tomorrows?

'When the hell do I get out of here? If ever?'

The word 'hell' set up a strange tremor. Out of the swirling phantasms there was suddenly a grey shape near his left shoulder, with an arm of absurd length raised as if in a salute — or a condemnation.

'Look, I have to get out of here sometime.' Was the shadowy figure listening? 'I can't stay here forever.'

'Why not?' It was no more than a whisper.

'It can't go on like this. I'd rather be dead.'

The arms of the shadow reached out impossibly far, embracing the bed and the ward and what lay beyond, then curved into a tight, cold embrace, eternally possessive.

'But where do you suppose this is?'

The grip relaxed. Eternal monotony lay ahead.

'Your date of death?'

7

The Svengali variations

It was on the first repetition of the minor theme that the viola player's long bronze hair began to distract him. Those glowing strands ought not to have fallen over her shoulder on the downward stroke of the bow. Not over her bare shoulder like that, at that point. It was out of tempo. Unsettling.

He found himself calculating when the next swing of hair, as fine as the horsehairs of her bow, would come. It ought to make a flourish at the start of the recapitulation, where the famous *sforzando* kicked the theme into a new dimension, but . . . no, she had anticipated it, and the swing of the hair added emphasis on the wrong beat. He wanted to call out to her, tell her to put her head back, so that the hair would whisk away and leave her shoulder bare again, glistening under the lights.

Gleaming even more brightly under those lamps rigged up in front of the altar was the bony head of the first violinist, like that of a skull, gaunt and demanding hushed respect. The second violin was a young man with an earnest smile, his eyes widening in amazement at his own skill in getting the phrasing right. The cellist was a grey-haired woman who glowered down at her bow as if daring it to go crooked and humiliate her.

The girl belonged in another world.

When the four players stood up and bent their heads to acknowledge the applause, at last she got the right balance. Her hair fell gracefully forward, and her right hand sketched an elegant arc as she swept it up and back, and bowed again and smiled.

He took a long time driving home, in no hurry to open his own front door and let himself into the nothingness inside.

The woman he had married ten years ago without thinking was in her usual position, facing the television. She pointed the remote control to turn the volume down and glanced indifferently over her shoulder. 'A nice concert?'

'A recital,' he corrected her. 'Just a quartet. Not bad. But the acoustics in that kirk are a bit dismal.'

She turned the volume back up again.

A week later he chose a channel himself in spite of her wanting to watch her usual soap. The quartet was appearing on a Border Television programme. But it wasn't the same. Studio sound and lighting were infinitely better, but everything was in two dimensions. The girl's face was beautiful but flat, her bowing did not thrust out at you. Her movements went stiffly from side to side.

And this other woman was here with him, souring the atmosphere. It was impossible to appreciate any of the nuances in the music with such a dissonance in the room. Yet it wasn't her fault. She just couldn't understand; never would understand. There were times when he felt quite guilty about having married her, when she was simply not up to it.

In the third movement's sprightly

ländler she said: 'Why do they keep coming back to that girl? She's not even the one playing the tune, is she?'

She knew as little about music as she did about camera angles. Of course any cameraman would keep coming back to that rapt face, that bare arm, that shoulder beginning to sparkle gently with sweat under the studio lights.

The weekend paper advertised another live performance as part of a chamber music festival in the Usher Hall in Edinburgh. It was miles from here, along that winding road under the Pentlands which he avoided whenever possible. His wife was baffled that he should change his mind for the sake of a string quartet.

'What's so special? You could always buy a CD and no' fash yourself dragging along there.' Then a possibility stirred. 'You could take me. We could stay a night in some hotel there, and I can do some shopping next day.'

She was trying hard. He ought to welcome the gesture. But he said: 'You wouldn't like it. You know how you get sick in the car, anyway. Better stay at home and treat yourself to one of those old Elvis DVDs.'

Music had been going on in his head while she spoke. That was the pattern nowadays. She would go on talking about prices in the local supermarket and about the vandals who had smashed windows in the Castle Hotel, and he would nod; and even though she probably realized he wasn't listening, she couldn't possibly imagine those other sounds which were putting up a defence inside his head — the sound of the owl hooting from Janácek's *Down an Overgrown Path*, the shuddering, piled-up discords accompanying the murder of Lulu in Alan Berg's opera . . .

He had tried to book a seat close to the platform, but the nearest he could manage was three rows back. It would require intense concentration for him to help her, to communicate the right gestures to her. Because that was what she needed. Soon there would grow an understanding between them. Silently he sent her a message to tell her he was here, concentrating.

And even from this distance she saw him. This time she really did become aware of him. Looked at him, looked away, and then back, worried.

He had to stop her worrying, so that she could devote herself single-mindedly to the smooth progression of notes.

Sixteen bars into the first *Allegro* she looked back at him, scraped a sour note, and jerked her gaze back to her music stand. Mentally he reproved her, but tried to convey as he leaned forward and stared between the heads in front of him, staring into her face, the message that he understood her need for encouragement. He was with her all the way. He would give her the strength to overcome a few technical problems. It didn't help that she was looking away, keeping her neck at an awkward angle as she avoided looking at him.

She really must learn not to be shy.

During the interval he tried to find a way of getting near to her, to chat and put her at her ease while he conveyed the support she needed. But there were officious little men barring the way, refusing to allow access to the players. All he could do was strain to help from a distance during the Ravel quartet and smile sympathetically as she took her bow and glanced nervously at him — probably because she had been aware of that quite ugly grace note, certainly none of Ravel's doing, in the last movement.

She really would have to learn what he could offer her.

He felt her beside him as he drove back late that night. He would have liked to stop and put a consoling arm around her shoulders. Bare shoulders, on a cold night like this.

The woman in his home was watching some late-night spy film. Without bothering to turn the volume down she asked if he'd had a nice time, and he answered just as indifferently, while an unexpected thread of a Bach chaconne whispered across his mind, conjuring up a brief vision of a girl with bronze hair dancing, keeping his memory of the evening still alive beneath the suffocating weight of banality.

Several weeks went by without any

announcement of recitals in the press or on television. Then he came across a small poster in the local tourist office advertising a performance in the library of a stately home outside Linlithgow.

The quartet was starting with Mozart's K458, the 'Hunt' Quartet, and after the interval would tackle Shostakovich's 12th Quartet. He was not at all sure how he would be able to help her through the Shostakovich, a composer he had little knowledge of. The best thing would be to have a word with her in the interval, when she could tell him briefly about any technical problems she had already encountered at rehearsal.

Seating arrangements were fairly informal, and he was able to move a chair to the end of the front row.

When the four instrumentalists came in from the side door of the library, to the usual spattering of welcoming applause, she was at once aware of him. He smiled reassuringly. She tossed her head so that the glow of her hair seemed to enfold and blend with the deep, glossy brown of the viola's body.

The Mozart went jubilantly on its way without much need of his intervention. He caught her eye several times, but did no more than nod encouragement.

In the interval he left his seat as the applause was dying away, and tried to follow her out through the door between the towering bookshelves.

The death's-head face of the quartet's leader stooped towards him, and the lean body came between him and the doorway.

'I'm sorry, sir, but the public are not allowed beyond this point.'

'I just want a word with your violist. Put her mind at rest. A few suggestions about certain aspects of — '

'We all appreciate having devoted followers in the audience.' The smile was skeletal. 'We're grateful for your continued support. But to put it tactfully, sir, we really would appreciate it if you didnae stare quite so intently at our Kirstie.'

Our Kirstie, indeed! Did the man not realize she wasn't his, or anybody else's. Save for the one she needed, the one she would have to turn to in the end. He said: 'I'm trying to help. She needs a sort of sympathetic sounding-board, you know.'

'Not from you, sir. You'd be doing her a favour by leaving her alone. Not staring quite so hard. It does put her off.'

That Saturday he bought a CD of the quartet, plus a second viola, playing two of the Mozart string quintets. He was sure he could hear which viola was Kirstie's, shimmering through the texture of the piece.

His wife was getting uneasy. 'What on earth are you getting into your head? That look of yours. Going to get into trouble again, are you?'

Trouble? That belonged in the past.

He had been music master at an academy in Fife. As well as teaching, it was expected of him that he should take part in school concerts and parents' days. Malicious blockheads had forced his dismissal after accusing him of relations with a fifteen-year-old when he was simply teaching her the fingering of the second piano part in the Milhaud duet, *Scaramouche*. It was hushed up, yet wherever he turned for employment somebody seemed to know about it.

No more academic posts, then. At last he found a job as a piano tuner. Not many people had pianos to tune nowadays, but there was just enough work in an instrument supplier's showrooms, follow-ups after a sale, and the occasional preparation for some minor celebrity's solo recital or concert performance.

Even then the lies followed him around.

A girl came into the sitting room one day while he was tuning the new upright her parents had bought for her. She watched, edged closer, and tempted him into letting her try playing a simple duet with him. He had his arm round her shoulder, trying to direct her left-hand fingering, when the mother came into the room.

'That's enough of that. Get out of this house.'

From then on his work was confined to part-time employment in the showroom.

Now, inspired by the secret rapport he felt building up between Kirstie and himself, he took to playing the piano for himself again.

'What's come over you?' The woman's usual timid whine was growing ugly, jarring with its false harmonics. 'You'd do better learning some proper pop music, go out to some gigs or ceilidhs or whatever, make us some decent money.' Then, rasping: 'You're wanting to be at it again, aren't you? At the young lasses again?'

Why had he married this person? Proximity, when she was working as a dinner lady at the school. Ignoring the jokes about her and about her exploits with boys in the sixth form. Yet she was the one who'd had the bloody nerve to sneer at him because of the lies they all told about his attitude to young, uncontaminated, virginal girls.

He practised feverishly to leave no room for her in his mind. Room only for a radiant girl with talent, with understanding, edging shyly and then more boldly into his dreams and planning the duets they would play when they appeared together.

He spotted an announcement about a charity recital at which she was to play three Schumann pieces and the F-minor sonata by Brahms, in the viola version rather than the original for clarinet. This was surely an omen. He bought a copy of the Brahms and practised even more devotedly than before, wrestling with the problems the composer seemed to be maliciously posing, marking some awkward moments of fingering with a red pencil until the piano score seemed to be covered with erratic bloodstains. At night Kirstie came to him in dreams in which they were both real and awake, and they rehearsed together until they had achieved perfection.

The night before the recital he went to bed early, making sure he got a good rest before tackling the challenging task ahead.

The forecast was for snow. And so it turned out.

He had known all along what would happen. The pianist booked for the recital phoned through from her mobile to say she was stuck in the snow on the way to the art gallery where the recital was to take place. The charity organisers were about to apologise to the audience and refund their money when he stepped forward and offered to partner Kirstie in the Brahms, of which he assured them he knew every note and nuance.

Of course she was shy and uncertain at first. A blush ran down her neck and faintly tinged that exquisite left shoulder. But when the organisers appealed to her, she warily agreed to let him join her. And the two of them knew that this was what she had really been waiting for. Her face gave nothing away as she tuned up, but he could sense from deep inside her the eagerness to be with him and release the passion they shared.

They carried off the challenging first movement with a fine flourish, so that the audience defied convention and applauded. In the second they had become two lovers, united in the languorous beauty of it, her body swaying towards him and back again, lilting into a new provocative rhythm when they reached the viola's threes over the piano's twos, then a switch of the configurations between the instruments, like an erotic reversal of sexual positions. They were making love, not in the way other vulgar folk made what they called love. Making love in music, wedded to it, pulsing with it until the hair fell away from her shoulder and all the rest of her naked body was radiant with desire.

Nothing could go wrong now.

Until the woman erupted, flinging herself through the audience, screaming obscenities, snatching the viola from Kirstie's hand and waving it above her husband's head.

He was reaching out for her throat, to stifle that voice once and for all, when he woke up.

'What the hell's the matter with you?' she was squawking. 'All that shouting and thrashing about. You filthy weirdo — treating yourself to wet dreams now?'

It was blasphemy. To be dragged back from euphoria to find all that beauty contaminated by the presence of this creature in his bed . . .

'You've interrupted our performance.' A great sob burst from him. 'Have you no taste at all?'

He put his hands round her throat again, finding it real and fleshy this time, and began squeezing; but then found he couldn't go on with it, and let her drag herself away, spluttering. 'You're pathetic.' She was almost jubilant in her anger. 'Really pathetic.'

When it was light he left the resentful, mumbling lump in the bed, showered, went downstairs, put the kettle on, and switched the portable from Radio 1 to the local station. There were warnings of gale force winds off the Irish Sea, and dangerous driving conditions over high ground. The northbound M74 was blocked by a three-car accident near Junction 12, with a 10-mile tailback.

And news had just come in that the talented Lanark viola player, Kirstie Kinnear, had died suddenly while rehearsing for a charity recital which she was to have given this evening, but which must now be cancelled. No cause of death had yet been established, but it was possible she had had a stroke as a result of recent overwork. An appreciation of her playing would be given in a programme later in the week.

He sat for a long while on the kitchen

chair, letting the tears come. He was the only one who could possibly understand what had happened. He had been torn away from her just as they were reaching the peak of their ecstasy, and she had died of a broken heart.

When the tears had ceased, he dried his eyes and then closed them, waiting. If he kept his eyes closed, Kirstie would come to him. She needed him more than ever now. From now on there would be no interruptions. They would be unashamed lovers, in love with music, while her bronze hair fell over her naked shoulder, the thrust of her bow intensified, and she smiled radiantly at him as they success-fully tackled a tricky passage in one of the Mozart sonatas.

With his eyes still closed, he urged Kirstie to come into the room. Out of this frowsty kitchen, into a shared dream of their own snug little rehearsal room where they would be together forever. Somehow that was how it had all been meant to turn out. Nobody else would understand; but then, there didn't have to be anybody else. No audience would ever be needed. It was to be their own wonderful, eternal secret.

'I suppose it'd be too much to expect you to bring me a cup of tea?'

He tried to shut out the voice from above, tried to shut out the expression he knew all too well would be on her face.

He switched over to Radio 3, and at once, as if it were a personal message, the rich nostalgia of Martinu's Viola Rhapsody-Concerto engulfed him. And now there was another face, forming in the shadows of the cold morning. The one he had been waiting for. He smiled, knowing that she'd had to come to him.

But it was a distorted face. Some shapes in the light were playing tricks on both of them. She was staring at him with hatred. And when she spoke, her thin voice was out of tune, rasping a perverse discord against the Martinu theme, a mockery as twisted as her lips and her hunched left shoulder.

Why couldn't you have left me alone?

He held out imploring arms to her, trying to bring her into focus and into the harmony that had to exist between them.

You killed me.

And now there was the other woman, halfway into the room, still in her crumpled nightdress.

'What are you staring at? Seen a ghost?'

He had longed for the ethereal Kirstie to be with him, close to him, for ever. But not this foul parody of her. And not with the flesh and blood creature between them, always between them.

This time when he reached out and got his grip, it was real. This time his hands closed on the real thing, this time squeezed and squeezed and did not let go until the foul, fleshy creature was sagging and slumping to the floor.

Dead now. Eliminated.

The discords clashed and shrieked in his head. He had silenced the worst of them but still there was this howl of lamentation.

Kirstie, denouncing him . . .

He had longed for their music never to stop.

Why couldn't you have left me alone?

It wasn't ever going to stop.

8

The Lorelei Hunger

He went through the magazine page by page, but this time couldn't find her. He blew against the sides of the pages in case two had stuck together. Still she refused to appear.

They must have dropped the campaign. How long did they run such promotions before changing the model, or changing the whole approach?

How did one set about finding her again?

If Edwin Blackett had been a thrusting businessman with top city connections, he could presumably have contacted the firm behind the product, and through them tracked down the advertising agency, and found some roundabout way of arranging a meeting with the woman in the picture and playing it from there. But he wasn't. Edwin was a stooped, middle-aged dealer in second-hand books, knowing more about the market for valuable limited editions than about the mass production, circulation and advertising revenues of lavishly coloured magazines.

He waited an anxious fortnight for his wife to collect the next colour supplement, and when she was out of the room flipped through it to the section where the picture usually appeared — the beginning of the fashion pages, just after the food articles. Again she was missing.

Silly to get worked up about it. Silly to become obsessed with a picture of some woman he could never hope to meet, and would not be able to cope with even if they should run across one another: a warm-skinned, sweet-smelling woman with shoulders rising exquisitely from a sleek wave of fine blue silk nightdress, with her *casque* of deep bronze hair and those dark green eyes staring out of the page not at the reader but into some remote dream

And how could he know from that two-dimensional glossy page that she would be sweet-smelling?

Of course she must be. The sort of wife

he longed to have. Making love to her would be so much easier, so sweet and gentle and satisfying, and afterwards she would slip back into her unruffled blue nightdress and go to sleep beside him. And she wouldn't snore and gulp spasmodically the way Marjorie did.

So unlike those other models cluttering up the pages of all the magazines nowadays in what they called the Season's Collections. 'Collections' at any rate was the right word: assemblies of unrelated bits and pieces, a strip of orange material hanging from one shoulder, snarled up in a wide belt above a dangling skirt which looked like a length of discarded sacking. Skinny legs sticking out beneath as the scrawny creatures minced towards the camera, scowling. Why were none of them ever allowed to smile; or were they physically incapable of it?

The beautiful, poised, mature woman in the blue nightdress was always smiling. Caught on camera with a smile that you just had to believe as genuine, always there.

And now she had escaped.

Perhaps they were going to run the nightdress advertisement only alternate fortnights from now on.

He reached yet again for the latest issue and turned the pages for the tenth — or fifteenth? time. She was always here, just at the end of the foodstuffs . . .

All at once it struck him. The page numbers didn't match up. Page 52 should be followed by page 53. Instead, it was page 55. He fingered the edge again, blew again; and still found himself with a gap. One leaf had been very carefully torn out, leaving not a mark — but loosening another page further on in the binding.

Someone had removed that very special pose.

It was inconceivable that Marjorie should have torn it out. Suspecting him of gloating over that picture, and taking it on herself to deprive him of it? No, she would have gone about it much more clumsily than that. Wouldn't have been able to resist confronting him with her knowing little leer and starting a silly little row. She had a habit of letting fly at random, interrupting whatever he might be doing or thinking — any peg giving her an excuse to blunder across his unspoken thoughts — and then pretending to be sorry, she hadn't known he was *thinking*, how could she have been expected to know he was *thinking*?

'Getting distracted from your stuffy old catalogues?' He could almost hear her voice now. 'Something with pretty pictures in it for a change? Better watch your blood pressure, at your age.'

All right, so he preferred his neat little unfussy black-and-white catalogues and the accumulation of book lore that lay behind them. The special language and shared mysteries of the antiquarian book trade enchanted him. The very first time he had come across the word 'incunabula' he had fallen under its spell. That was music in itself, representing all the mystery and yet reliability that he craved.

It was pure chance that he had idly picked up one of those very different magazines and skimmed dismissively through it — dismissive, until he first came across that one advertisement.

Marjorie and her friend Beryl swapped

magazines and Sunday colour supplements once a fortnight. Marjorie's regular contribution was a consumer magazine. Its articles about the way people got fleeced by unscrupulous salesmen and shopkeepers confirmed her general suspicions of everybody in the world around her. She was always accusing the local corner shop of cheating her, of the gas people deliberately misreading the meter, and everybody in local and national government taking bribes and fiddling expenses.

The periodical frequently featured travel sections. 'Why do we never go on holiday to somewhere like Lanzarote?' She would squeeze a little fold into the top of each page ready to snap it over to new desirable destinations. 'They're doing these special flights. We could afford one of these, don't say we couldn't. I mean, look, only five pounds to get to Venice.'

'Five pounds one way,' Edwin would point out, 'and it doesn't say what it'll cost you to get back.'

Beryl Darby's main contribution to their swap was this glossy home magazine, which aroused more of Marjorie's longings. And aroused something unexpected within Edwin Blackett. What excuse could he find for getting his hands on an issue before that page got ripped out?

Mrs. Darby usually dropped in late on Saturday mornings on her way back from the weekend's shopping. He made a bold decision.

'Got to take this package to the post.'

'I'll take it when I go to the Co-op,' Marjorie called from the kitchen.

'A fussy customer, this one. The post goes early on a Saturday. Don't want to risk missing it.'

He picked up Marjorie's magazine from the hall table along with some of her letters to be posted — letters ordering, no doubt, all sorts of household discount catalogues and holiday brochures — and was out of the house before she could ask any awkward questions.

* * *

Beryl Darby was a large woman, with a surface not so much brassy as over-glossy.

Her eyes were slightly protuberant, her teeth very bright and even, and her voice not exactly bossy yet unvaryingly loud. Three different ropes of brassy jewellery clanked together round her neck, over the puckered skin of her throat, and down over her lumpy bosom.

'Well I never. To what do I owe the pleasure? I'm afraid we don't have any valuable old editions of Shakespeare or whoever for sale.'

He held the magazine out awkwardly. 'Just thought as I was passing I'd save you or Marjorie the trip.'

'Well, come in. Fancy a cup of coffee?'

'Er, no. Not really. No thanks. I was just passing, and — '

'Yes, you've just said that.' She cocked her head sideways and looked at Edwin with what he supposed was known as an arch expression. 'But come in anyway. I'll have to go and fetch the other mag. Exchange no robbery, isn't that what they say?'

When he had the magazine in his hands he made a show of idly flipping through it, but before he could risk too obviously checking whether that page was in its right place in this issue there was the slam of a door and her husband stomped in.

Joseph Darby — known to everyone, on his own insistence, as Josh — was, if anything, larger and brighter and louder than his wife, with a mottled red face and insistently matey laugh. You felt he would be more at home with plastic-wrapped magazines from the top shelf than with his wife's sort of reading matter.

'Hello, running the errands now, eh? Got to get the prize crossword in on time?'

Edwin frequently did the crossword in *The Guardian* on his morning train, but had never bothered to check whether there was one in this magazine. He could only mumble something, but it didn't matter: Josh was not one to expect answers to his cheerful booming.

On the train that next Monday morning Edwin was in fact folding the newspaper to the crossword puzzle page when Josh slumped heavily into the seat beside him.

Edwin had always avoided the man on

the few occasions when they used the same train. Fortunately these were rare. As far as he knew — and this information came entirely from Marjorie, who could well be muddled in the detail — Joseph Darby was rep for a firm manufacturing leather goods of various kinds, which Edwin assumed to mean shoes and belts and briefcases like the one he was carrying right now. It meant he didn't travel regular commuters' hours; but today he was here, and making a point of seeking Edwin out and squashing into the seat beside him.

'Off to open the shop, Eddie?' He opened his briefcase and took out a folded page sliced from a magazine. 'This what you were looking for, old lad?' He unfolded it and held it in front of Edwin. 'Fancy ripping that nightie off her, eh?'

It was the missing page.

Edwin forced a laugh. He wasn't capable of trotting out chirpy, meaning-less phrases. But Josh wasn't even waiting for an answer. 'Here, keep it, old lad. I've already got one for my collection. Amazing where they show up, though,

these birds. What about *this*. Then . . . ?'
He dug deeper into his briefcase, tugged
out a garishly covered magazine, and
flipped through it to a double-page
spread. 'Get a load of her *this* time, then.'

There were three women and two men
sprawled across the centrefold. Edwin
tried to look casually at them, then looked
away, then was drawn back. He tried an
easy laugh. It wasn't by any means that
easy.

The beautiful woman wasn't looking
aloof and enchanting in a sheer silk
nightdress. She was wearing only a couple
of leather straps twisted round her breasts
and in a contorted loop between her legs.
At the same time she was contriving to
spread those legs and offer herself to one
of the men, while a dark, greasy-looking
girl clambered over him from another
angle.

That face he had found so cool and
beautiful and refreshing . . . such a
change from the squalor and ordinariness
of everyday life . . . such an ideal,
untouchable yet so delicious to be
yearned for . . .

It couldn't be.

'Fancy a session like that, old son?' Josh's voice was rasping on, right by his ear yet miles away. 'Time you had a fling in the outside world. Exercise the old whatnots. Good for your health, you know.'

Edwin looked out of the window and kept on looking out.

Within another twenty minutes he was mercifully on his own, as usual. He went through the reliable, reassuring business of opening his shop and settling in, happy to deal with a knowledgeable customer or equally happy to set some postal enquiries in motion. He glanced along his reassuring shelves and let the faded bindings of his stock blank out the visions Josh Darby had conjured up.

He reached for a volume of legends, a book which would bring in some profit when he found the right customer but which he would in the end be reluctant to sell. He found it soothing to take a leisurely journey through the old plates with their visions of fairies and legendary monsters. He would be happy if somebody came in to browse round those shelves; happy if he was left alone until lunchtime.

The phone rang. Reluctantly he reached for it. 'Blackett Books.'

'This is Mr. Edwin Blackett?'

'It is.' And he was about to rattle off his usual incantation that no, he didn't want free entry into a new cannot-lose competition, and no, he did not have the time to answer their consumer survey, when the silky voice went on: 'It has been destined that we should meet, has it not?'

'Who is this speaking? And how did you obtain my number?'

'You know who it is. I'm sure you do. You've seen me, wondered about me. And now the time has come for us to meet.'

He put the phone down. Whatever this new scam was, he had no intention of falling for it. Then he fretted over it. That voice . . . it went so well with the unforgettable photograph of the woman in blue. He tried to wrench his mind away on to business. For once he was offhanded with a customer, one of those time-wasting customers who had read about the two volumes of the Border

Papers increasing in value and his uncle happening to have left him two of them in their original binding and what would they be worth? The sort of thing Edwin might on a good day enjoy assessing and bargaining over. But now he was eager to get the man off the premises so that he could pick up the phone again and dial 1471.

'You had a call at eleven forty-two a.m. today. The caller withheld their number.'

Of course. The con men always did.

A con woman . . . ?

* * *

Next morning he was mercifully on his own in his usual compartment. On his own, that is, except for the usual complement of young men with their flickering iPads, or Kindles, or whatever the damned things were called. The abomination of it all, the destruction. Everything served up in snippets. None of the joys of searching the rewards of the noble, reliable past. Edwin opened the latest catalogue he had received from a dealer in Antwerp, but found it hard to concentrate. He wrenched his head around to stare fretfully out of the window. The train was slowing for the tight bend that would take it across the river and into the town. He knew every inch of the scene spread out there — the huddle of warehouses, the brief open space of a school playground, and then the huge billboard facing the railway line and clamouring for attention from passengers who were so familiar with it that it probably had no impact whatsoever. For the last couple of weeks it had advertised a BA plane soaring up against a vast blue sky. Today the background was still blue, but in the foreground were the head and bare shoulders of a woman — *the* woman.

The leaflet slid from Edwin's fingers to the floor. He groped to pick it up while still keeping his gaze fixed on the inexplicable vision. There was no wording, no name of the advertiser — just that face, those shoulders, seeming to grow larger and larger as if to embrace the train; yet at the same time dissolving into a remote haze.

And there was music. Not the jangle from those cheap little nuisances across the aisle, but haunting, alluring voices reaching without any need of mass-made transmitter into Edwin's mind. Into his mind and his alone — he was sure of that.

Then they had crossed the river, and the terminus and his usual day lay ahead of him.

He half expected another phone call. Expected it . . . longed for it . . . dreaded it?

On the homeward journey he struggled to find a seat on the opposite side from his usual place, so that he could lean back a bit and have another look at that billboard. But the hallucination had disappeared.

Because of course it must have been a hallucination. Absurd. He had to dismiss it. No future in that kind of daydreaming.

★　★　★

Another morning, and Josh again appearing and this time pushing his way into a seat facing Edwin. 'Doing a booming trade in historic erotica this week, old son?'

'Not my speciality, I'm afraid,' Edwin managed.

'Pity. Dirty books are better for you than dusty books any day.'

'I've never handled that sort of thing.'

'Speaking of handling things . . . '

Josh laid his latest gadget on the table between them, turning it to face Edwin. 'Amazing what you can pick up on your travels these days. Special wavelength, of course. Reserved for connoisseurs, you might say.'

Edwin wasn't at all sure he wanted to look. But Josh was prodding it aggressively towards the edge of the table, and his neighbour was snatching glances at it. Reluctantly Edwin pushed it closer to the window, at an angle.

There she was. Just her face this time, smiling wistfully beside one border of a narrow block of type. At an angle on the other side of the column, a darker woman was leaning forward as if to leap through the frame: her mouth open, the lower lip slack, silent, yet obviously having just said something brash and suggestive.

Josh leaned forward to press a button, like someone showing a child how to manipulate a new toy.

Words sprang up in bold type.

'Book now for the voyage of your dreams. Escape to the reality of your deepest fantasies on the MV Ligeia. The dream cruise for wide-awake men.'

'What d'you say?' Josh pressed another button for details to unroll down the cramped screen. 'Coming with me?'

The following paragraphs detailed costs and timetables for cruises — 'for a select few connoisseurs' — on the 'romantic Loch Yearn, the haunt of dream partners and the reality of fulfilment.' Edwin had only occasionally glanced at dating agency ads in his newspaper and would then hastily look for something else to read, but this one did seem to him like a very advanced, more suggestive specimen than most.

He forced a grin and pushed the thing back across the table.

Only when they were jostling their way through the morning crowds on the platform did Josh say insistently: 'I did ask you if you were game to come along.'

'Me? What nonsense.'

'To meet that woman — not worth it? Fight a duel over her, the two of us, maybe? Great experience. 'Reality of your deepest fantasies' — doesn't that grab you?'

'We couldn't . . . I mean, I couldn't . . . '

'This loch. I've checked on it. Damn great reservoir — flooded a whole valley to make it. What used to be one piddling little village got swallowed up in the bottom of it. Used to be called Kirkcraig. But if that ad's anything to go by, what's left is well stocked with juicy females. And of course some very refined ones. To suit every taste. Come on, old son. I'll be there to hold your hand — unless you want to let it roam, which'd be OK with me.'

They came out into the open and Edwin muttered some platitude before hurrying across the street towards the safety of his little shop.

For once Josh was on the evening train as well, persisting.

'Got to have a story that should satisfy

the womenfolk, right? Look, I have to make some calls up there over the Border. Maybe interest these folk as well in some whips and specialised leather goods.' If they had been sitting side by side, Edwin had an uneasy feeling that Josh would have been nudging him. 'Look, there's this place Wigtown not that far away, calls itself The Book Town. You must have been there.'

'Once or twice.'

'Well then, there we are. You come along with me as a guide. You know the territory. Help one another out. If either of us needs help, eh?'

'I don't think I could — '

'You can choose how far to indulge. How close to get, and then . . . well, it'd be up to you. No hassle.'

'I do know that part of the world, but I honestly can't imagine what they mean by that — '

'Do you good to get away for a bit. Put your foot down, tell the old woman you need a breath of fresh air after sitting in there choking in the dust from those books of yours.'

In fact Marjorie couldn't bring herself to object. She looked as if she didn't believe a word of what he was saying, yet it was so unlike him that she was too puzzled to know where to thrust her usual immediate put-down.

'Well, if you two are going to get up to no good . . . ' She stared, at a loss. 'I suppose it'll be something to talk about later.' She was almost daring him to shock her, but at the same time scoffing at the mere idea of it.

★ ★ ★

The landing stage was no more than a small floating pontoon at the end of a lane which had once led down to the village before the waters flooded in over its houses, chapel and pub. A narrow gangplank led on to the deck of the cabin cruiser, which looked hardly big enough to accommodate more than a dozen people. Yet when Edwin and Josh boarded, there seemed to be far more than that in the lounge bar, and others leaning on the rail outside waiting to watch the crew cast off and set out on to the tranquil waters of the man-made loch.

'Well,' boomed Josh, 'where's the talent? Where's these daydreams we've paid for?'

Edwin looked around the main cabin. Between the wide windows were murals of rocky riverbanks, and one tapestry of a seascape with wave-splattered rocks. Shapes that from one angle might be meant to convey subtleties of the light, from others became the bodies of women clinging to the rocks and reaching out, yearning, calling. On the largest expanse, in the bulkhead towards the bows, the scene was clearly that of the Sirens singing their desperate demands to the tormented Odysseus tethered to the mast of his ship.

There was music. Not pop jangles piped from speakers in the corners, but music suffusing the whole atmosphere, music whose provocative beauty he had fleetingly heard just that once before, in the train. At the same time he remembered a quotation from one of the many books he had leafed through not for their literary content but their possible antique market value: 'What song the sirens sang . . . '

Then came deeper notes: a more urgent bass throb from the engines, settling into a lulling rhythm as the boat slid away from the shore. Sunshine raked blindingly from the water like stabbing searchlights. Edwin turned away towards the starboard side, half closing his eyes and shielding them with his hand. When he opened them, it was as if one of the paintings on the wall had come to life.

A girl was there, smiling at him. She had long flaxen hair, and was wearing a scarlet silk chiffon dress, which rustled with every faint movement of her body within. Her pale lips were slightly parted, with the faintest glimmer of teeth behind them, slightly pouting, waiting to open . . . so that the teeth could bite?

'Welcome aboard.' Her voice was husky and suggestive. 'Now we're afloat, every-day restrictions no longer apply. You are free to make your own choice, in your own time.' Her fingers rested lightly on his arm, turning him towards the entrance to a companionway stair. At the lower end was what looked like a swimming pool. Only it was too impossibly large for this small craft carrying it. Impossible. A cunningly projected illusion? A film of naked women diving, swimming under water, surfacing, laughing and tempting a man — some man, any man — to come in and join them.

And there, suddenly, was Josh Darby. A fat porpoise, spluttering and sploshing about, making a grab for a girl missing her but getting his hands on another, a dark woman with streaming dank black hair. They wallowed and wrestled in the water, and her mouth closed greedily over his, swallowing his lips, gulping him in. Edwin could somehow feel the pulse of it, and like Josh found himself fighting for breath.

'No.' It was all he could find to say.

'Take your time.' The fingers squeezed his arm. 'I'm sure we have someone you'll find to your taste.'

'I think there's been some mistake.'

'No, this is quite usual.' The voice was still a husky, tempting purr. 'Over the centuries we have had to adapt, but there will always be men like you to keep us alive. You are here, as you always have been, to rejuvenate us. Take your time. But since you have answered our call, you must make your choice.' And then, throatily: 'Or be chosen.'

He turned away, just as he had turned away from Josh's pictures in the train, and looked out of the window. They were approaching an island. He had seen no sign of this from the shore.

Again there was music. A young man was leaning against a long polished stanchion, playing a guitar. To Edwin he looked a typical modem youngster, slipshod in tatty shirt, torn denims and sandals. But the music he was playing wasn't the pop clangour that might have been expected. Instead it had all the wistful echoes of an old folk song.

Edwin grasped the chance to shake off the suggestiveness of what he had just been exposed to. 'Good morning.' It sounded too absurdly polite, everyday. But that was what he needed. Wrench everything back to normal. 'Edwin

Blackett.' He held his hand out. 'Lovely morning, isn't it?'

The strings left a brief, quivering echo. 'Jamie Dunbar.'

'And what brings you here today?' It was the closest Edwin could get to asking why a healthy young man should need to be among middle-aged men paying a fare to be taken to . . . well, taken where? He was still wondering what he had let himself in for.

'She sent for me.'

Not, surely, the same temptress? Too mature for him, not his type.

'My girlfriend.' Jamie Dunbar swung the guitar back over his shoulder. 'I haven't seen her since . . . since she disappeared. But she's been in touch.' His voice was as plaintive as the chords of his music. 'We thought we'd lost her altogether. But she's here somewhere . . . waiting for me.'

'Lost her?'

They were side by side, looking out across the waters. Except that Jamie was looking down below the surface rather than towards the hazy island.

'Down there. She came from the village they drowned to make the reservoir. That's how it got that weird name: Loch Yearn. Folk always talking about going back where they belonged. And we thought she must have done something silly. Got lost somehow.' He took a deep breath. 'Drowned.'

'But now you think . . . '

'It's crazy. I was just reading this email I was getting from a . . . well, *another* girl I was just getting to know.' He smiled sheepishly. 'And . . . well, this one from my old girlfriend comes in, sort of blotting the new one out and saying she has to meet me. I've got to come on this trip to meet her.'

Edwin went on staring at the island, which seemed to come no closer although the boat's engine was still thrusting it energetically onwards.

'Yes,' said an insinuating voice close to his left ear. 'Just a memory of where we come from.'

This time it was the real woman, the one who had been no more than a distant fantasy but whom he had let himself be lured into meeting.

Her hair glowed like sun-sparked amber. She was wearing seashell earrings, trailing long green and brown tendrils like very fine seaweed. Her dress was a rippling velvet as green as her eyes, with tucks of shadow which were pale rather than dark, as if her skin were showing through slits in the material. But when he thought how much he preferred that first picture he had seen of her, somehow this dress was immediately transformed to meet his demand, and her shoulders emerged ravishingly into a fresh flood of sunlight.

She said: 'I knew you would come. But you don't care to join in the pleasures of the pool?'

He took a deep breath. 'I didn't come here just at random. Just to . . . well, get mixed up with anybody and everybody.'

'You are discriminating. Which is why I called you.' Her smile was deliciously mocking. 'You took your time answering! But now you are here. We are together. You are ready to be alone with me and not disappoint me? You are in love with what I am prepared to ask of you, yes?'

'Well, I . . . that is . . . ' Damn it, why couldn't he speak, act, reach out and put his hands on those shoulders, move closer?

'If you want to be away from the others, it presents no problem. Of course you prefer the privacy of my retreat. My cavern has been prepared for you.'

Without his noticing, the haze had lifted from the island and now it was clear-edged. There were shapes — human shapes? — moving on it, and others apparently sprawled out, resting. He forced out yet another trite remark: 'You live here permanently? I mean, over there?'

'We live here, all of us, in the way we have always lived. More restricted than our lives used to be, but we can exist. Exist' — it was more a wailing entreaty than an explanation — 'so long as we are well fed. We need the perpetual rejuvenation we were used to. That is why you are here: why you have been sent for.'

Sent for? Lured, he thought with a sickening lurch in his stomach.

'Fate has decreed it this way. For us — the Sirens, the mermaids, the selkies, those who must forever draw men into the waters. Or out onto the rocks and islands of temptation. Yes.' Her hand was on his arm, stroking rhythmically. 'Aren't you honoured to be chosen to feed me?'

'Feed you? I don't see how I can . . . I mean' — even as he spoke he knew it sounded ridiculous — 'isn't there a meal included in the booking?'

She waved at the tapestry. 'We need . . . *replenishing*. We can no longer exist in the old ways. Our singing can no longer be heard above the discords of transmitters belching forth from the pleasure cruisers, the constant traffic, the speedboats, the aircraft carrying our livelihood far away above us. People forever staring into petty things they hold in their hands, not looking around them, not listening. Men no longer venture bravely into the unknown, because there are no longer any unknowns on this earth. So we had to swim away from our old polluted seas and our rivers, to flee across hundreds of weary sea miles until we found our way upstream to this new lagoon. Found our new haven, where we can fulfil our destinies.' Her fingers slid down and tightened around his wrist. 'We have always existed, immortal, feeding men's dreams. But there has to be a price to pay. We, too, need feeding.'

'Look, I don't quite get this — '

'When we reach my cavern you will understand. You have surely read of us as legends in those old books you are so fond of. But we are more than legend. Real and richer than the dry paragraphs in any of your books. So wonderful for you.' Her face was close to his. 'You may call me by name. I am Lorelei.'

Light from every side was still playing on her cheek and bare shoulder. A dancing impertinence of fingers of light, touching, feeling. Yet the smoothness he had visualised from her photograph was becoming a thin, transparent layer. Under it was glistening bone, a skull shining through the skin yellowed not by light but by age. Incredible age.

Over her exquisite shoulder he again glimpsed that phantasmal pool below them. Only now the waters were in a dark turmoil, and Josh was not so much yielding to an embrace as struggling to free himself. The woman clamped herself even more tightly, her legs scissoring round him, her whole body impaled on him and gripping him agonisingly, squeezing every drop of sustenance out of him, her nails biting into his back so that the blood ran under her nails and down her fingers.

And there were others in the whirlpool of stupefying lust. Men who had answered the advertisement and come to fulfil their dreams. The creatures were swarming over them, struggling to retain human shape. Those arms which the gullible prey had thought would be so warm and soft and yielding were cold, the skin becoming like that of some reptile, slithering over and round them, but never relaxing their hungry grip.

She said: 'Of course you want no part of that. You will find it more beautiful with just the two of us in my cavern.'

'You mean out there? On that island?'

'Deep, deep into it. I come up for the warmth of the sun, and food, when I must. To call men to me.' Those fingers had ceased to caress. They were tightening, grasping, demanding. 'We shall be alone there. You will rejoice in what you can give me. Your appetite and mine, they will be one.' Her breath was warm on his cheek. 'Sometimes,' the mesmeric voice murmured on, 'we find a lover worth keeping. Not to be greedily used up all at once. To be kept . . . and savoured at intervals.' But that in breath was becoming rank, a stench of rotting seaweed and a foulness from depths beyond human comprehension.

And surely those shapes on the island were no longer human? They looked like discarded costumes, the deflated skins of what had once been living beings. Skins sucked dry, tossed aside, no longer of any use.

He forced himself to look away from the island, away from this creature clinging to him. Down there in the depths, was that a glimpse of the little bell-cote of the chapel? Mud swirled and blurred the image, then cleared for a moment of writhing, thrusting limbs. How many of these creatures were swimming in and out among the empty door and window frames of the old abandoned houses?

What might have been no more than a swirl of the current began shaping itself into the body of a girl, a shape which grew more beautiful as it rose through the surface of the loch and leapt aboard like a fish throwing itself onto dry land. But as she flapped and gasped for breath she was reaching out triumphantly towards young Jamie Dunbar as he came out on deck. He bent towards her; she reared up; they swayed in what might have been the movement of a sinuous new dance; and then, together, they went over the rail and down, down into the streets of the silent yet still pulsating village.

'A selkie who had outstayed her time on land,' said the creature called Lorelei dismissively. 'She will have difficulty getting him to adapt to our ways down there.' She was beginning to sound impatient. 'Come, now. Shall we take ourselves away? I chose you because I thought you would be worthy. You should be honoured.'

The promised dream had become a nightmare. He struggled to wake up. He must concentrate on waking up, reaching for the glass of water beside his bed, and soothing Marjorie's drowsy grumbling.

'Come on,' she rasped. The fingers had become claws, the skin of her face was beginning to peel away in oozing strips from the gaunt skull. 'We're running it too close. *Come* to me. You *must*. Come *on*.'

There was sudden uproar from below decks. Some men were laughing, some protesting, others sounded as if they were fighting drunk; and the voices of the women were a clash of implacable siren songs distorted by the discords of voices turning sour, losing their fervour.

As if under panic orders, the boat shuddered into a tight turn and raced towards the shore. It was much closer than their steady outward progress would have suggested.

'You fool. Worthless fool.' Lorelei was screaming on and on. 'Unworthy. You could have been one of the favoured ones. Now be damned. You will never be allowed to forget. Be damned into eternity.'

He found that Josh was beside him,

strangely shrunken, grabbing his arm to steady himself. Somehow they were ahead of the others, scrambling ashore and starting to run without knowing how far they would have to go before they were safe, out of hearing of the sirens' song and the sirens' appetites.

Safe. Would they ever be safe?

★ ★ ★

Marjorie Blackett had asked a dozen or more questions without getting any answers that satisfied her before going off to exchange the usual magazines with Beryl Darby. When she came back she looked, for the first time in their married life, disturbed by the possibility of hitherto unsuspected quirks in her husband.

'What on earth did you do to Josh Darby?'

'I didn't do anything to Josh.'

'But whatever the two of you got up to — '

'We didn't get up to anything.'

'Well, whatever it was,' Marjorie persisted, 'he looks a lot the worse for wear.'

He had nothing to say to her. And nothing to say to Josh when they met again on the train for the first time since their escapade.

This time Josh did not come plumping himself down forcefully beside Edwin or slap things on the table with a flourish. He stooped, eased himself into the seat, and grinned apologetically. They finished the journey without him uttering a word. How could he keep moving at all? He was an empty bag of skin, all the inner life sucked out of it. Gutted and thrown back. Tossed back onto dry land. But with just enough energy left to keep it moving, maintaining a pretence of being alive.

Edwin Blackett was still, he prided himself, Edwin Blackett. He opened his shop, cast an eye along his stock, and waited for the post. Things he had ordered would arrive in the usual way. He would assess them, make his decisions, send in his entries to the most important catalogues, make decisions.

Making decisions . . .

He found he couldn't concentrate. With a book in his hands he couldn't appraise it, was incapable of even opening it.

He no longer dared to open a magazine.

Was she rotting away by now? Could he have been the one to save the incomparable beauty of her? Was he to be forever racked by the guilt of her death?

Or was she like the shapes he had seen, the carapaces discarded on the land?

Still capable of resuscitation?

Beryl Darby brought the usual magazine in, but made a point of speaking only to Marjorie, glancing apprehensively at Edwin and then scuttling out. When she had gone he turned to the fateful page; but it was now advertising something for young stick insects.

He found himself telling Marjorie that there had been some unfinished business back in that distant Book Town, and of course it was a nuisance, but he couldn't get people to make any sense on the phone, and he'd have to go back and sort it out.

She didn't believe him; but somehow was too scared to argue.

* ★ ★

The landing stage was even smaller than he remembered, no more than a few planks jutting out from the bank. The boat moored to it was a very small cabin cruiser, certainly not made for more than ten passengers. It didn't look as if it was used very often. The tourist trade hadn't been any great success yet.

And the island within which Lorelei fed on her willing sacrifices . . . and the gutted carcases were cast aside?

Only a small brick and concrete turret lifted its conical cap above the centre of the reservoir: probably a pumping shaft of some kind.

It began to rain. Very gently at first, sweeping a subdued drumming across the surface of the loch. Through the tap-dancing of the raindrops came bursts of a light-hearted melody, a tune that became a rippling chorus of laughter, voices bubbling up from the sunken village.

It might have been an invitation to Edwin Blackett to join in. But it wasn't.

He had been rejected. As he stumbled

away, the rain and the pulsations from the depths grew more forceful, more derisive.

They were laughing at him. And would go on deriding him, laughing at him forever.

THE END

We do hope that you have enjoyed reading this large print book.

Did you know that all of our titles are available for purchase?

We publish a wide range of high quality large print books including:

Romances, Mysteries, Classics
General Fiction
Non Fiction and Westerns

Special interest titles available in large print are:

The Little Oxford Dictionary
Music Book, Song Book
Hymn Book, Service Book

Also available from us courtesy of Oxford University Press:

Young Readers' Dictionary
(large print edition)
Young Readers' Thesaurus
(large print edition)

For further information or a free brochure, please contact us at:
Ulverscroft Large Print Books Ltd.,
The Green, Bradgate Road, Anstey,
Leicester, LE7 7FU, England.
Tel: (00 44) 0116 236 4325
Fax: (00 44) 0116 234 0205

FEAR BY INSTALMENTS

John Burke

Mike Merriman's big band and his vocalist, Ingrid Lee, are extremely successful. However, returning from touring America, they are questioned by reporters concerning their relationship. Worse still, when Mike's wife disappears, Ingrid is subjected to a campaign of vengeance. The threats and attacks grow in savagery. At home or on stage, Ingrid suffers potentially murderous persecution. Meanwhile, Mike can only strive to put an end to the terror building up so remorselessly — the *Fear by Instalments*.

QUEER FACE

Gerald Verner

On the trail of a jewel robber, Superintendent John Brent from Scotland Yard lies in wait, with the police, outside a riverside country house — the thief's next anticipated target. But, avoiding arrest, the armed robber fatally shoots Brent and escapes onto to his boat. When the launch is found, a single thumbprint is the only clue to the owner's identity. Brent's policeman son, vows to find the man responsible — the man he will come to know as 'Queer Face'.

LEGIONNAIRE FROM TEXAS

Gordon Landsborough

Sometimes a serving legionnaire will crack under the brutality of life in a desolate waste and then desert. But the big Texan plans to desert for his own reasons. Why has he joined the foreign legion under an assumed name? And why has an American newspaper-woman, disguised as an Arab girl, joined a caravan crossing the Sahara? When they meet and discover they both share the same secret agenda, they are unaware of their impending life and death struggle to survive . . .

THE WOLVES OF CRAYWOOD

V. J. Banis

Dark tragedy strikes the three Cray brothers: two girls have been brutally torn apart by vicious beasts — the countryside around Craywood blazes with the legends of the were wolf. No one believes that a man could have caused such horror . . . Gaye reluctantly answers her sister Susan's call for help and learns that Susan blames Walter Cray for the killings. Nightmare follows nightmare, and soon Gaye herself is marked for death! Can anyone stop *The Wolves of Craywood*?